"I expected your dad."

"He had other obligations. So I'm your man."

In your dreams, buddy.

Although there was no reason, really, that being within fifty feet of the man should raise every hackle she possessed. Wasn't as if there was any history between them, save for an ill-advised—and thankfully unrequited—crush her senior year of high school when grief had clearly addled her brain and Noah had been The Boy Every Girl Wanted. And, rumour had it, got more often than not. Well, except for Roxie.

Twelve years on, not a whole lot had changed, as far as she could tell. Not on Noah's part, and— apparently— not on hers.

Which, on all counts, was too pathetic for words.

Dear Reader,

Anyone who's ever had more than one child (or been part of a family with multiple siblings) will recognise Noah Garrett as The One Who Makes His Mother's Heart Stop on a Regular Basis—the kid who fears nothing and nobody, the child most likely to come home bruised and bloody. Or with something gross or scary. And yet inside that daredevil kid often lurks a very sensitive soul, one that harbours doubts and fears he wouldn't dream of confessing to anyone…or even to himself.

Like, for example, being scared to death of falling in love? Oh, yeah—even tough, cocky Noah has an Achilles' heel, and her name is Roxie Ducharme…a gal who can definitely teach him a thing or two about overcoming adversity. And who, whether she means to or not, forces Noah to reassess everything he's believed about himself up to this point.

Because only in the arms of a strong woman does a man become all he can be.

Enjoy!

Karen

HUSBAND UNDER CONSTRUCTION

BY
KAREN TEMPLETON

MILLS
BOON

First published in Great Britain 2011
by Mills & Boon, an imprint of Harlequin (UK) Limited,
Eton House, 18-24 Paradise Road, Richmond, Surrey TW9 1SR

© Karen Templeton-Berger 2011

ISBN: 978 0 263 89417 2

23-0312

Harlequin (UK) policy is to use papers that are natural, renewable and recyclable products and made from wood grown in sustainable forests. The logging and manufacturing processes conform to the legal environmental regulations of the country of origin.

Printed and bound in Spain
by Blackprint CPI, Barcelona

Since 1998, RITA® award-winner and Waldenbooks bestselling author **Karen Templeton** has written more than thirty books. A transplanted Easterner, she now lives in New Mexico with two hideously spoiled cats and whichever of her five sons happens to be in residence.

To my guys
who've been there for me
literally and figuratively in every way that matters.
My gratitude for all of you knows no bounds.

Chapter One

If you asked Noah Garrett's mama to describe her son in one word, she'd immediately say, "Daredevil," accompanied by the heavy sigh of a woman who'd seen the inside of the E.R. far, far too often.

Even as an infant, the boisterous New Mexico thunderstorms that sent his older brothers diving into their parents' bed made him coo in delight. While other toddlers howled in fright if a dog licked their faces, Noah would howl with glee. As he got older, no tree or roof was too high to climb—or jump off of—no bug too big or ugly to examine, no basement too creepy to explore, no night too dark to sneak out into when he was supposed to be asleep. And woe betide the erstwhile playground bully who dared mess with Noah. Or any of his brothers.

So the churning gut as Noah said, "I'll do it," while staring his father down across the banged up desk in the tiny, cluttered office was highly uncharacteristic.

Not to mention unsettling. Especially as that churning gut had nothing to do with his father, who, yes, made Noah crazy on a regular basis but did not frighten him in the slightest. Behind him, on the other side of the open door, power saws ripped and hammers pounded and a half dozen employees shouted to each other in Spanish over the constant noise, more secure in their jobs than they probably had any right to be. And aside from his father, nobody was more determined to give them reason for that security than Noah.

Even if it meant sacrificing his own in the process.

Rubbing his chest, Gene Garrett lowered his big-bellied self into the rickety, rolling chair behind the desk to wrestle open the perpetually stuck top drawer and rummage inside for heaven-knew-what.

"Good of you to offer," he muttered as he searched, "but Charley's *my* friend. He'll expect me to do the estimate. Not you."

"Except," Noah said, "aside from the fact that Charley's not even going to be there, I'm gathering this is going to involve a lot more than new cabinets. Not to mention you're up to your eyeballs with that order you're installing in Santa Fe next week—"

"And you've got the Jensen project," Gene grunted out as he leaned sideways, the drawer swallowing up his bulky forearm.

"Finished that up two days ago. Next objection?"

His father looked up, his thick, dark brows bouncing over his gold-rimmed glasses like a pair of goosed caterpillars. "Could be a big job."

"Not any bigger than the Cochrans', I don't imagine. And I handled that just fine."

Gene again contorted himself to peer into the depths of

the drawer, then reinserted his arm. "You and *Eli* handled it just fine. So no harm in waiting a week, until I'm free."

Despite his determination not to let the old man get to him, annoyance zinged through Noah. "And you know full well it's a miracle Roxie got Charley to even think about fixing up the place," he said, over a zing of an entirely different nature. "So she probably wants to present him with the estimate as a done deal. Strike while the iron's hot. You said yourself the house is in pretty bad shape—"

"Which is why," Gene said, finally righting himself, a half-empty bottle of Tums clutched in one scarred, beefy hand, "I can't let just anybody handle it."

This honoring your father thing? Sometimes, not so easy. "I'm not 'anybody,'" Noah said patiently. "I'm your son." Even when his father shot him a pained looked that said far more than Noah wanted to hear, he refrained from pointing out exactly whose idea it had been to begin with, to branch out from woodworking into full-scale remodeling services, anyway. Instead, he simply said, "Only trying to take the load off you."

One paw straining to pry the childproof cap off the bottle, Gene flashed a frown in Noah's direction. "Don't need you or anybody else to take the load off. You still work for me, remember?"

"Like you'd ever let me forget. Give me that," Noah said, leaning across the desk to snatch away the half-strangled bottle before his father hurt himself trying to get the damn thing open. "So let me put it another way—either let me run with this, now, or risk Charley's changing his mind and we lose the job altogether."

The bottle easily—and gratefully, Noah surmised—relinquished, Gene linked his hands over his belly. "And

I don't suppose Charley's pretty niece has anything to do with you wanting this job?"

Focusing *real* hard on the bottle top, Noah snorted. "Roxie? Doubt she even likes me." Which, judging from her reaction to him the few times they'd run into each other since her return to Tierra Rosa a few months back, probably wasn't that far from the truth.

Never mind that the first time Noah'd clapped eyes on her he'd felt as if somebody'd clobbered him with a telephone pole. A reaction he'd never had to another female, ever. He didn't understand it, he sure as hell didn't like it, and no way was he about to admit that after a lifetime of rushing headlong into potential danger without a second thought—or, in most cases, any thought at all—the idea of working with Roxanne Ducharme made him break out in a cold sweat.

"There some reason you get up her nose?" Gene said, in the long-suffering way of a man whose sons had more than tested the concept of unconditional love.

"Not that I can recall." Which was the truth. And you'd think her completely unexplained antipathy would at least somewhat mitigate the telephone-pole-upside-the-head thing. You'd be wrong.

"Not even back in high school?" said Mr. Dog-with-a-Bone across from him, and Noah thought, *And you're going down this road why?* They were talking a dozen years ago, for cripes' sake.

"She was only there for that one year. And ahead of me at that."

"Never mind that you lived right across the street from each other."

"Doesn't matter." Noah handed back the open bottle, thinking that even with his crazy schedule back then, working afternoons and weekends at the shop whenever he didn't have practice or a game, he must have seen her at some point. But damned if he could remember. "I doubt we exchanged two dozen words the entire time. She's a potential client," he said, directly meeting his father's eyes. "Nothing more."

After an I-wasn't-born-yesterday look, Gene tipped the bottle into his palm, shook out a couple of antacids. "Just remember—" he popped a pill into his mouth, crunched down on it "—the past always comes back to bite us in the butt."

Meaning, Noah wearily assumed, the string of admittedly casual relationships which somehow translated in his father's mind into Noah's overall inability to commit to anything else. Like, say, the business. Noah's knowing it backward and forward—having never worked at anything else from the time he was fourteen—apparently counted for squat.

Before he could point that out, however, Gene said, "Now, if you want to get Eli in on this one, too—"

"Forget it, Eli's so sleep-deprived on account of the new baby he's liable to pass out on Charley's sofa. Dad, I can handle it. And hey—what's up with popping those things like they're candy? You okay?"

Rubbing his breastbone, Gene softly belched before palming the few valiant, light brown strands combed over an age-spotted scalp. "Other than having two weeks' worth of work left on a project due in six days? Sure, couldn't be better. That burrito I wolfed down an hour ago isn't doing me any favors, either." Then he sighed. "And your mother's about to drive me nuts. And don't you dare tell her I said that."

Aside from the fact that his parents' making each other nuts was probably the glue holding their marriage together, considering how aggravated Noah was with his father for refusing to admit he needed help, he could only imagine how his mother felt. Still, sometimes playing dumb was the smartest choice. "About what?" he asked mildly.

Gene pulled a face. "About taking some time off." Releasing another belch, he rattled the Tums. "Days like this, a guy needs his buddies. But it's not like this is the first tight deadline I've pulled off."

"And if you don't start taking better care of yourself it might be your last."

"Oh, Lord, not you, too—"

"You even remember the last time you went on vacation?"

"Sure. When we went to visit your mother's sister in Dallas. Couple years ago."

"Five. And visiting family does not count. *And* you called home a dozen times a day to check up on things."

"I did not—"

"Got the cell phone records to prove it. And anyway, whether you think you need down time or not, you ever stop to think maybe *Mom* might like to get away? With you? Alone?"

After giving Noah a "Who *are* you?" expression, Gene grunted. "Donna's never said one word to me about wanting to go anywhere."

"When does Mom ever ask for anything for herself?" Noah shot back, suddenly annoyed with both of them, for loving too much and asking too little and putting up with far more crap from their kids than any two parents should have to. At which point he wasn't sure who he was, either. "Frankly, I don't think she even remembers how. If she ever did." Emotion clogged Noah's throat. "Yeah, she's worried about you. With good reason, apparently," he said, nodding toward the Tums.

Father and son exchanged a long look before Gene said, "I had no idea you cared that much."

Honest to God. "Maybe if you looked past your own issues with me every once in a while," he said softly, "you would."

Leaning back in his chair again, Gene regarded Noah with thoughtful eyes, as a light November snow began to halfheartedly graze the grimy office window. Then, on a punched-out breath, he said, "I just don't understand—"

"I know you don't. And sometimes I'm sorry for that, I really am. Other times…well. It'd be nice if you'd find it in yourself to accept that I'm not like you. Or the others. Now," he slipped his hands into his front pockets, "what time's that appointment? At Charley's?"

After another long moment, his father said, "Two."

Noah checked his watch, then snatched his worn leather jacket off the rack by the office door, grabbed a clipboard from the table under it. "Then I'd better get going."

As he walked away, though, his father called behind him, "You call me if you've got any questions, any questions at all. You hear?"

Only, as he struck out for Charley's house—barely two blocks from the shop—the glow from the small victory rapidly faded, eclipsed by the reality of what he'd "won."

Lord, Roxie would probably laugh her head off—assuming she'd find humor in the situation at all, which was definitely not a given—if she knew Noah's brain shorted out every time he saw her.

That his good sense had apparently gone rogue on him.

Not that Noah had anything against family, or kids, or even marriage, when it came down to it, he thought as he rounded the corner and headed up the hill he and his brothers had sledded down a million times as kids. For *other people.* If his brothers and parents were besotted with wedded bliss, cool for them. As for his nieces and nephews...okay, fine, so he'd kill for the little stinkers. But since, for one thing, he'd yet to meet a gal who'd hold his interest for longer than five minutes, and for another, *he was perfectly okay with that,* his reaction to Roxanne Ducharme was off-the-charts bizarre.

God knows, he had examples aplenty of healthy, long-term relationships. Knew, too, the patience, unselfishness, dogged commitment it took to keep a marriage afloat. Thing was though, the older he got, the more convinced he became he simply didn't have it in him to do that.

To *be* that, he thought with another spurt of gut juice as he came to Charley's dingy white, 1920s-era two-story house, perched some twenty feet or so above street level at the top of a narrow, erratically terraced front yard. In the fine snow frosting the winter-bleached grass and overgrown rosebushes, it looked like a lopsided Tim Burtonesque wedding cake. Even through the snow, the house showed signs of weary neglect—flaking paint, the occasional ripped screen, cement steps that looked like something big and mean and scary had used them as a chew toy.

He could only imagine what it looked like on the inside.

Let alone what the atmosphere was likely to be.

Noah sucked in a sharp, cold breath, his cheeks puffing as he exhaled. Maybe he should've given Roxie a heads-up, he thought as he shifted the clipboard to rummage in an inside pocket, hoping he'd remembered to replenish his stash. *Yes.* Although he'd quit smoking more than five years ago, there were still times when the urge to light up was almost unbearable. This was definitely one of those times.

Thinking, *Never let 'em see you sweat,* he marched up to the front door, plastered on a grin and rang the bell.

* * *

Ding-dong.

Wrestling a dust bunny with a death grip from a particularly ornery curl, Roxie carefully set the tissue paper-smothered Lladro figurine on her uncle's coffee table and went to answer the front door…only to groan at the sight of the slouching, distorted silhouette on the other side of the frosted glass panel.

Thinking, *Road, hell, good intentions, right,* Roxie yanked open the door, getting a face full of swirling snow for her efforts. And, yep, Noah Garrett's up-to-no-good grin, glistening around flashes of what looked like a slowly-savored chocolate Tootsie Roll pop.

Eyes nearly the same color twinkled at her when Noah, a clipboard tucked under one arm, lowered the pop, oblivious to the sparkly ice bits in his short, thick hair. His dark lashes. The here-to-forever shoulders straining the black leather of his jacket—which coordinated nicely with the black Henley shirt underneath, the black cargo pants, the black work boots, sheesh—as he leaned against the door frame.

"Hey, Roxie," he rumbled, grinning harder, adding creased cheeks to the mix and making Roxie wonder if dust bunnies could be trained to attack on command. "Dad said Charley needed some work done around the house?"

"Um…I expected your dad."

A shrug preceded, "He had other obligations. So I'm your man."

In your dreams, buddy.

Although there was no reason, really, why being within fifty feet of the man should raise every hackle she possessed. Wasn't as if there was any history between them, save for an ill-advised—and thankfully unrequited—crush in her senior year of high school, when grief had clearly addled her brain and Noah had been The Boy Every Girl Wanted. And, rumor had it, got more often than not. Well, except for Roxie.

Twelve years on, not a whole lot had changed, far as she could tell. Not on Noah's part, and—apparently—neither on hers.

Which, on all counts, was too pathetic for words.

"Kitchen first," she muttered as she turned smartly on her slipper-socked foot, keeping barely ahead of the testosterone cloud as she led Noah through the maze of crumbling boxes, bulging black bags and mountains of ancient *Good Housekeeping*s and *Family Circle*s sardined into the already overdecorated living room.

"Um…cleaning?" she heard behind her.

"Aunt Mae's…things," she said over the pang, now understanding why it had taken her uncle more than a year to deal with her aunt's vast collections. Even so, Roxie found the sorting and tossing and head shaking—i.e., a box marked "Pieces of string too small to use." Really, Aunt Mae?— hugely cathartic, a way to hang on to what little mind she had left after this latest series of implosions.

Except divesting the garage—and attic, and spare room, and shed—of forty years' worth of accumulated…stuff… also revealed the woebegone state of the house itself. Not to mention her uncle, nearly as forlorn as the threadbare, olive-green damask drapes weighing down the dining room windows. So Roxie suggested he spruce up the place before, you know, it collapsed around their heads. Amazingly, he'd agreed…to think about it.

Think about it, go for it…close enough.

However, while Roxie could wield a mean paint roller and was totally up for taking a sledgehammer to the kitchen cabinets—especially when she envisioned her ex-fiancé's face in the light-sucking varnish, thus revealing a facet to her nature she found both disturbing and exhilarating— that's as far as her refurbishing skills went. Hence, her giving Gene Garrett a jingle.

And hence, apparently, his sending the one person guaranteed to remind Roxie of her penchant for making Really Bad Decisions. Especially when she was vulnerable. And susceptible to…whatever it was Noah exuded. Which at the moment was a heady cocktail of old leather and raw wood and pine needles. And chocolate, God help her.

"Whoa," Noah said, at his first glimpse of the kaleidoscope of burnt orange and lime green and cobalt blue, all suffused with the lingering, if imagined, scents of a thousand meatloafs and tuna casseroles and roast chickens. She adored her aunt and uncle, and Mae's absence had gouged yet another hole in her heart; but to tell the truth the house's décor was intertwined with way too many sketchy memories of other sad times, of other wounds. Far as Roxie was concerned, it couldn't be banished fast enough.

"Yeah," she said. "'Some' work might be an understatement."

Just as this estimate couldn't be done fast enough, and Charley would sign off on it, and Noah or Gene or whoever would send over their worker bees to make magic happen, and Roxie would get back to what passed for her life these days—and far away from all this glittery, wood-scented temptation—and all would be well.

Or at least bearable.

The Tootsie Roll pop—and Roxie—apparently forgotten, Noah gawked at the seventies-gone-very-wrong scene in front of him, clearly focused on the job at hand. And not even remotely on her.

Well…good.

"And this is just for starters," Roxie said, and he positively *glowed,* and she thought, *Eyes on the prize, cupcake.*

And Noah Garrett was definitely not it.

Despite the stern talking-to Noah'd given himself as he hiked up all those steps about how Roxie was no different from any other female, that he'd never not been in total control of his feelings and no way in hell was he going to start now— The second she opened the door, all dusty and smudgy and glowering and hot, all he knew was if the Tootsie Roll pop hadn't been attached to a stick he would've choked on the blasted thing.

Noah'd stopped questioning a long time ago whatever it was that seemed to draw females to him like ants to sugar, it being much easier to simply accept the blessing. So if he was smart, he mused as he pretended to inspect the butt-ugly cabinets, he'd do well to consider Roxie's apparent immunity to his charm, or whatever the hell it was, a blessing of another sort. Because if she actually gave him the time of day he'd be toast.

While he was pondering all this, she'd made herself busy sorting through a couple of battered boxes on the dining table on the other side of the open kitchen—more of her aunt's stuff, he surmised—affording him ample opportunity to slide a glance in her direction now and then. Maybe the more he got used to seeing her, the sooner this craziness would wear off. Back off. Something.

Long shot though that might be.

So he looked, taking in a cobweb freeloading a ride in a cloud of soft, dark curls that were cute as all hell. The way her forehead pinched in concentration—and consternation, he was guessing—as she unloaded whatever was in those boxes. The curves barely visible underneath the baggy purple K-State sweatshirt. Then she turned her back to him, giving him a nice view of an even nicer butt, all round and womanly beneath a pair of raggedy jeans pockets.

She jerked around, as if she could read his mind, her wide eyes the prettiest shade of light green he'd ever seen, her cheeks all pink, and for a second Noah thought—hoped—the world had righted itself again. As in, pretty gal, horny guy, what's to understand? Not that he'd necessarily act on it—one-sided lust was a bummer—but at least he felt as if he'd landed back in his world, where everything was sane and familiar and logical.

Except then she picked something off the table and walked back into the kitchen. "Here, I made a list of what needs doing so I wouldn't forget," she said, handing him a sheet of lined paper and avoiding eye contact as if she'd go blind if she didn't, and suddenly her attitude bugged like an itch you can't reach.

As Noah scanned the list—written in a neat, Sharpie print that was somehow still girly, with lots of question marks and underlinings—bits and pieces of overhead conversations and whispered musings, previously ignored, suddenly popped into thought. Something about losing her job in Kansas City. And being dumped, although nobody seemed clear on the details. With that, Noah realized that grinding in his head was the sound of gears shifting, slowly but with decided purpose, shoving curiosity and a determination to get at the truth to the front of his brain…and shoving lust, if not to the back, at least off to one side.

"This goes way beyond the kitchen," he said, and she curtly nodded. And stepped away. This time Noah didn't bother hiding the sigh. She wanted to hate him? Fine. He could live with that. Heck, he'd be happy with that, given the situation. Just not without reason.

Roxie's brows dipped. "What?"

"There some unfinished business between us I'm not remembering?"

The pink turned scarlet. Huh. "Not really. Anyway," she said with a pained little smile, "the kitchen is the worst. But the whole house—"

"Not really?"

If those cheeks got any redder, the gal was gonna spontaneously combust. "Figure of speech. Of course there's nothing between us, unfinished or otherwise. Why—?"

"Because it's kind of annoying being the target for somebody else."

Dude. You had to go there.

Roxie's jaw dropped. *"Excuse me?"*

Noah crossed his arms, the list dangling from his fingers, his common sense clearly hightailing it for parts unknown. "God knows, there's women with cause to give me dirty looks. If not want my head on a platter." At her incredulous expression, he shrugged. "Misunderstandings happen, what can I say?" Then his voice softened. "And rumor has it you've got cause to be pissed. But not at me. So maybe I don't appreciate being the stand-in, you know?"

After a moment, she stomped back to the dining room to dig deep into one of the boxes, muttering, "Now I remember why I left. The way everybody's always up in everybody else's business."

"Yeah. I think that's called *caring,*" Noah said, surprised at his own defensiveness. Even more surprised when Roxie's gaze plowed into his, followed—eventually—by another tiny smile, and he felt as if his soul had been plugged into an electrical outlet. Damn.

"No, I think that's called being nosy," she said, and Noah chuckled over the *zzzzzt.*

"Around here? Same difference."

The smile stretched maybe a millimeter or two before

she dropped onto a high-backed dining chair with a prissy, pressed-wood pattern along the top. "It's a bit more complicated than that, but...you're right. And I apologize. For real this time. It's not you, it's..."

She rammed a hand through her curls, grimacing when she snagged the cobweb. "This hasn't been one of my better days," she sighed, trying to disengage the clumped web from her fingers. "Sorting through my aunt's stuff and getting nowhere in my job search and thinking about...my ex—and trust me, it's not his *head* I want on a platter—" A short, hard breath left her lungs. "I feel like somebody's weed-whacked my brain. Not your fault you're the weed-whacker."

"I'd ask you to explain, but I'm thinking I don't really want to know."

"No. You don't." Once more on her feet, Roxie returned to the kitchen, leaning over the counter to scratch at something on the metallic, blue-and-green floral wallpaper over the backsplash. "I promise I'll be good from now on."

"That mean I have to be good, too?"

"Goes without saying," Roxie said, after a pause that was a hair too long, before her gaze latched onto his Tootsie Roll pop. "Got another one of those?"

Lord above. Noah had gotten tangled up with some dingbats in his time, but this one took the cake. Not even the cute butt could make up for that. Even so, this could shape up—heh—to be a pretty decent job, so he supposed he'd best be about humoring the dingbat.

"Uh...yeah. Sure." He dug a couple extras out of his pocket. "Cherry or grape?"

"Cherry," Roxie said, holding out her hand, not speaking again until it was unwrapped and in her mouth, her eyes fluttering closed for a moment in apparent ecstasy. Then, opening her eyes, she grinned sheepishly around the pop. Mumbling something that might have been "Cheap thrill," she slowly removed it, her tongue lingering on the candy's underside, her gaze unfocused as she dreamily contemplated the glistening, ruby-red candy on the end of the stick, which she gently twirled back and forth between her fingers. "Can't remember the last time I had one of these," she sighed out, then looked at him again, her pupils gradually returning to normal. "Well. Ready to see the rest of the house?"

Holy crap.

Lust run amok Noah could handle. Electric jolts he could ignore, if he really put his mind to it. But the two of them together?

This went way beyond unfamiliar territory. This, boys and girls, was an alternate universe. One he had no idea if he'd ever get out of alive.

If he even got out at all.

Chapter Two

The longer Roxie trailed Noah through the house, batting away the pheromones like vines in a jungle, the easier it became to see why the man had to fight 'em off with sticks. Not that he'd ever seemed to fight too hard. His reputation was well documented. But holy moly, the dude exuded sexual confidence by the truckload. As opposed to, say, herself, who did well to summon up enough to fill a Red Rider Wagon. On a good day.

Then she mentally smacked herself for giving in to the woe-is-me's, because nobody knew better than she that the road to hell was paved in self-pity. And, um, yearnings. Reciprocated or otherwise. Especially for a man she'd likened to gardening equipment.

Anyway.

"Wow. You weren't whistling Dixie about the condition," Noah said, practically leering at the peeling wallpaper. The worn wood floor. The disintegrating window sills—ohmigod, the dude looked practically preorgasmic as he fished a penknife out of his back pocket and tested a weak spot in a sill in the living room. Years of neglect eventually took their toll.

In more ways than one, Roxie thought, savoring the last bit of her cherry-chocolate pop as she tossed the bare stick in a nearby trash can. "How bad is it?"

Noah flashed her a brief smile probably meant to be reassuring. "Fortunately, most of the it seems to be more cosmetic than structural." Now frowning at the sill, he gouged a little deeper. "I mean, this is pretty much rotted out, but...no signs of termites. Not yet, at least." A stiff breeze elbowed inside the leaking windows, nudging the ugly, heavy drapes. "Windows really need to replaced, though."

"You can do that?"

"Yep. Anything except electrical and plumbing. That, we hire out." He glanced around, frowning. "Sad, though. Charley letting the house get this bad."

Out of the blue, a sledgehammer of emotions threatened to demolish the "everything's okay" veneer she so carefully maintained. "He didn't mean to. Basically, he's fine, of course, but his arthritis gets to him more often than he'd like to admit. Then Mae got sick and he became her caregiver...." First one, then another, renegade tear slipped out, making her mad.

"He could've asked for help anytime," Noah said quietly, discreetly looking elsewhere as he snapped shut the knife and slipped it back into his pocket. "My folks, especially— they'd've been more than happy to lend a hand. If they'd known."

Swiping at her cheeks, Roxanne snorted. "Considering neither Charley nor Mae said anything to *me,* this is not a surprise."

Noah's gaze swung back to hers. "You didn't know your aunt was sick?"

"Not for a long time, no. Although, maybe if I'd shown my face, or even called more often, I might have."

"You think they would've told you if you had?"

Her mouth pulled tight. "Doubtful."

"Then stop beating yourself up," he said, and she thought, *And you, stop being nice.* A brief shadow darkened his eyes. "My folks don't tell us squat, either. And all four of us are right here in town. In fact, a few years back my brothers and I figured out they were in the middle of a financial crisis they didn't want to 'burden' us about. Had to read 'em the riot act before they finally fessed up." He half smiled. "Keeping the truth from the 'kids' is what adults do."

A bit more of the veneer curled away, letting in a surprisingly refreshing breeze. "I guess." She sighed out. "I mean, even when I came home for Thanksgiving a couple of years ago and could sense something was off, that Charley was being more solicitous toward Mae than usual—and that was going some—they both denied it. I finally browbeat him into telling me what was really going on—" she swallowed back another threat of tears "—but whenever I suggested taking a leave of absence, or even coming for the weekends to help out, he refused." A humorless laugh pushed from her throat. "*Very* emphatically."

"Don't take this the wrong way…but Dad says Charley's known for being a little, ah, on the stubborn side."

"A *little?*" She chuckled. "Why do you think it took so long before he'd let me go through Mae's things? Or even think about fixing up the house? Although, considering it had only been the two of them for so much of their marriage, I honestly think they simply didn't want anything or anybody coming between them, even at the end. Especially at the end."

After a moment's unsettling scrutiny, Noah squatted in front of a worn spot on the flooring. "And that made you feel useless as hell, right?"

"Pretty much, yeah. But how—?"

"Like I said, I've been there." He stood, his fingers crammed into his front pockets, watching her, like…like he got her. And how ridiculous was that? He didn't even know her, for heaven's sake. The logic of which didn't even slow down the tremor zapping right through her. Well, hell.

"Maybe I should've been pushier, too," Roxie said, thinking she'd take remorse over this tremor business any day. "By the time your mother called me, Mae was nearly gone. And even then, even though Charley obviously couldn't handle things by himself that last week, I still felt in the way." She backed out of Noah's path as he moved into the dining room, rapping his knuckles once on Mae's prized cherrywood dining table before crossing to the bay window, a DIY project that hadn't exactly stood the test of time. "Like I was infringing on their privacy."

"Must be scary, loving somebody that much," he said to the window, and she had the eerie feeling hers wasn't the only veneer peeling away that day.

"Yes, it is," she said carefully, although her younger self probably wouldn't have agreed with him, when she still clung to the delusion that bad things happened to other people. "Then again, maybe some people find it comforting. Knowing someone's there for you, no matter what? A lot less scary than the alternative, I'd say."

Noah craned his neck to look up at her, a frown pushing together his brows.

"Sorry," she muttered, feeling her face heat. Again. "Not sure how things got so serious. Especially for your average estimate walk-through."

Getting to his feet, Noah's crooked grin banished the

heaviness in the room like the sun burning off a fog, sending Roxie's heart careening into her rib cage. "Oh, I think *average* went out the window right around the time you compared me to a weed-whacker. Besides…this is a small town. And your aunt and uncle were friends with my folks for years. So no way is this going to be your standard contractor/client relationship." He paused, looking as if he was trying to decide what to say next. "Mom and Dad've mentioned more than once how concerned they are about Charley."

Roxie smirked. "That he's turned into a hermit since Mae's death, you mean?"

"'Closed off' was the term I believe Mom used."

"Whatever. Again, I wasn't around to see what was happening. Not that I could have been." She sighed. "Or he would have let me. He tolerated my presence for a week after the funeral, before basically telling me my 'hovering' was about to push him over the edge."

"And now you're back."

"A turn of events neither one of us is particularly thrilled about."

"You think your uncle doesn't want you here?"

Once more rattled by that dark, penetrating gaze, Roxie sidled over to a freestanding hutch, picking up, then turning over, one of her aunt's many demitasse cups.

"I think…he wants to wallow," she said, shakily replacing the cup on its saucer. "To curl up with the past and never come out. I'm not exactly down with that idea. Frankly, I think the only reason he finally agreed to let me start sorting through Mae's things was to get me off his case."

"And *you're* not happy because…?"

Roxie could practically hear the heavy doors groaning shut inside her head. Talking about her uncle was one thing.

But herself? No. Not in any detail, at least. Especially with a stranger. Which, let's face it, Noah was.

"Several reasons. All of them personal."

His eyes dimmed in response, as though the door-shutting had cut off the light between them. What little of it there'd been, that is.

"So is it working?" he asked after a moment, his voice cool. "You trying to get your uncle out of his funk?"

"I have no idea. Opening up to others isn't exactly his strong suit."

A far-too-knowing smile flickered around Noah's mouth before he glanced down at the notes, then back at her. "To be honest…this is shaping up to be kinda pricey, even though I can guarantee Dad'll cut Charley a pretty sweet deal. And I haven't even seen the upstairs yet. I mean, yeah, we could paint and patch—and we'll do that, if that's what you want—but I'm not sure there'd be much point if it means having to do it all over again five years from now. But the windows should really be replaced. And the cabinets and laminate in the kitchen. We can refinish the wood floors, probably—"

"Oh, I don't think money's an issue," Roxie said, immensely grateful to get the conversation back on track. "Not that much anyway. I gather his work at Los Alamos paid very well. And he and Mae lived fairly simply. And there was her life insurance.…" Another stab of pain preceded, "Anyway. Wait until you get a load of the bathroom.…"

Feeling as if he'd gotten stuck in a weird dream, Noah followed Roxie up the stairs, the walls littered with dozens of framed photos on peeling, mustard-striped wallpaper. Mostly of Roxie as a baby, a kid, a teenager. A skinny, bright-eyed, bushy-haired teenager with braces peeking through a broad smile. Funny-looking kid, but happy.

Open.

Then her senior portrait, the bushiness tamed into recognizable curls, the teeth perfectly straight, her eyes huge and sad and damned beautiful. Almost like the ones he'd been looking at for the past half hour, except with a good dose of mess-with-me-and-you're-dead tossed into the mix.

A warning he'd do well to heed.

This was just a job, he reminded himself. And she was just a client. A pretty client with big, sad eyes. And clearly more issues than probably his past six girlfriends—although he used the term loosely—combined.

Then they reached the landing, where, on a wall facing the stairs, Roxie and her parents—she must have been eleven or twelve—smiled out at him from what he guessed was an enlarged snapshot, taken at some beach or other. Her mother had been a knockout, her bright blue eyes sparkling underneath masses of dark, wavy hair. "You look like your mom."

Roxie hmmphed through her nose. "Suck-up."

"Not at all. You've got the same cheekbones." He squinted at the fragrant cloud of curls a foot from his nose, and a series of little *pings* exploded in his brain. Like Pop Rocks. "And hair."

"Unfortunately."

"What's wrong with your hair?"

"You could hide a family of prairie dogs in it?"

If he lived to be a hundred he'd never understand what was up with women and their hair. Although then she added, "But at least I have no issues with my breasts. Or butt. I like them just fine," and the little *pop-pop-pops* become *BOOM-BOOM-BOOMS.*

Before the fireworks inside his head settled down, however, she said, "Mae and Charley really were like second parents to me. Even before…the accident. If it hadn't been for them I honestly don't know how I would've made it through that last year of school. All I wanted to do was hole myself up in my bedroom and never come out. Until Aunt Mae—she was Mom's older sister—threatened to pry me out with the Jaws of Life. So I figure the least I can do for Charley is return the favor."

"Whether he likes it or not," Noah said, even as he thought, *How do you live with that brain and not get dizzy?* Because he sure as hell was.

"As I said. And the bathroom's the second door on the right."

To get there Noah had to pass a small extra bedroom that, while tidy to a fault, still bore the hallmarks of a room done up for a teenage girl, and a prissy one at that—purple walls, floral bedspread, a stenciled border of roses meandering at the top of wall. None of which jibed with the woman standing five feet away. Except the room made him slightly woozy, too.

"You like purple?"

She snorted. "Aunt Mae wanted pink. I wanted black. Purple was our compromise. Didn't have the energy to fight about the roses."

"Somehow not picturing you as a Goth chick."

A humorless smile stretched across her mouth. "Honey, back then I made Marilyn Manson look like Shirley Temple. But…guess you didn't notice, huh?"

A long-submerged memory smacked him between the eyes, of him and his friends making fun of the clot of inky-haired, funereal girls with their raccoon eyes and chewed, black fingernails, floating somberly through the school halls like a toxic cloud. One in particular, her pale green eyes startling, furious, against her pale skin, all that black.

"Holy crap—that was you?"

To his relief, Roxie laughed. "'Twas a short-lived phase.

In fact, I refuse to wear black now. Not even shoes." Grimacing, Roxie walked to her bedroom doorway, her arms crossed. "I put poor Mae and Charley through an awful lot," she said softly, looking inside. "I even covered up the roses with black construction paper. Mae never said a word. In fact, all she did was hug me. Can you imagine?"

His own childhood had been idyllic in comparison, Noah thought as a wave of shame washed over him. Man, had he been a butthead, or what? "What I can't imagine, is what hell that must've been for you. I'm sorry. For what you went through, for…all of it."

"Thanks," she said after a too-long pause.

"So you gonna paint in there or what?" Noah said, after another one.

Roxie turned, bemusement and caution tangling in her eyes. "Why? Not gonna be around long enough for it to matter, God willing. So. The bathroom?"

Yeah, about that. Nestled in a bed of yellowed, crumbling grout, the shell-pink tiles were so far out of date they were practically in again. As were the dingy hexagonal floor tiles. And way too many vigorous scrubbings had taken their toll on the almost classic pedestal sink, the standard-issue tub bearing the telltale smudges where a temporary bar had been installed. And removed.

There was way too much pain in this house, like a fungus that had settled into the rotting wood, lurking behind the peeling wallpaper, between the loose tiles. Noah pressed two fingers into one pink square; it gave way—probably far more easily than the bad vibes clinging to the house's inhabitants.

At least he could fix the house. The other…not his area of expertise.

"Since the tile's crap, anyway—" He flicked another

one off. "Why don't we do one of those all-in-one tub sur-rounds? Although it wouldn't be pink."

Roxie leaned against the doorjamb. "I sincerely doubt Charley would miss the pink. Although…could we install grab bars at the same time?"

Noah got the message. "They're code now, so no prob-lem."

"Oh. Good." Roxie sighed. "Charley's far from decrepit, heaven knows, but I know he wants to live on his own, in his own house, as long as possible. So I'd like to make sure he can do that."

Noah looked at her. "Because you won't be around."

A dry laugh escaped her lips. "To be honest, when I was eighteen and stuck here…oh, Lord. I thought I'd been consigned to hell. It was one thing to come for vacations, but I couldn't wait to get back to the city. I love the energy, the way there's always something going on, the *choices*. Heck, I even like the noise. So no, I can't see myself calling Tierra Rosa home for the long haul. Besides, I have to go where the work is. Work in my field, I mean. And so far, I haven't even been able to find anything close by—"

"Roxie? You up there?"

Blanching, she whispered, "Crap. He wasn't supposed to be back for another hour!"

"Should I hide in the closet?"

"Believe me, it's tempting," she muttered, then pushed past Noah to call from the landing, "Up here, Charley. With…Noah Garrett."

"Noah? What the Sam Hill's he doing here?" Charley said, huffing a little as he climbed the stairs, only to release a sigh when he saw the clipboard in Noah's hand. "Ah." A bundle of bones underneath badly fitting khaki coveralls and a navy peacoat probably older than Roxie, the older man turned his narrowed gaze on his niece. "Thought you'd pull a fast one on me, eh? Guess I fooled you. No offense, Noah. But it appears the gal was getting a little ahead of herself—"

"But you agreed to let me get an estimate—"

"I *said* I'd think about it. Honestly." Again, his gaze swung to Noah, as if he expected to find an ally. "What is it with women always being in such a rush?" He glared at his niece. "Bad enough you act like you can't get rid of Mae's things fast enough, now you want to change everything in the house, too? And what's up with *you* being here and not your daddy?" he said to Noah, who was beginning to feel as if he was watching a tennis match. "You sniffing around Roxie, like you do every other female in the county?"

"For heaven's sake, Charley—!"

"I'm only here on business," Noah said, getting a real clear picture of what Roxie must be going through, dealing with her uncle every day. If it was him he'd be looking for out-of-town jobs, too. At the same time the near panic in the old man's eyes was so much like what he saw in his father's—that threat of losing control, of everything changing on you whether you want it to or not—he couldn't help but feel a little sorry for the guy. "Because Dad's tied up. And Roxie only has your best interests at heart, sir. To be honest, I'm seeing a lot of safety issues here. And the longer you put off fixing them, the worse they're going to get. And more expensive."

"Well, of course you'd say that, wouldn't you? Since it's you standing to make money off me—"

"Charley," Roxie said in a low voice, gripping his arm until, mouth agape, he swung his pale blue eyes to hers. "Listen to the man. The house needs work. A lot of work. And if you don't take care of it you're not going to be able to stay here."

Her uncle slammed his hand against the banister railing.

Which was missing a couple of stiles, Noah noticed. "I'm not leaving my house, dammit! And you can't make me!"

"Then let's get it fixed," she said gently but firmly, "or you may not have any choice in the matter, because no way am I letting you stay in a pit—"

"Choice?" Her uncle yanked off his snow-frosted knit cap and slammed it to the floor, freeing a forest of thick, white hair. "What kind of *choice,*" he said, wetness sheening his eyes, "is railroading me into something before I'm r-ready?"

"Oh, Charley…" On a soft moan, she wrapped her arms around him, her tenderness in the face of his cantankerousness making Noah's breath hitch. Then she let go and said, "I know this is hard. And you *know* I know *how* hard." She ducked slightly to peer up into his averted face, thin lips set in a creased pout. "But sticking your head in the sand isn't going to solve the problem. And we can't put it off much longer, since I have no idea when a job offer's going to come through. I'm trying to *help,* Charley. We all are."

Several beats passed before her uncle finally swung his gaze back to Noah. "It's really that bad?"

Catching Roxie's exhausted sigh, Noah said, "Yes, sir. It is."

Charley held Noah's gaze for another moment or two before shuffling over to a small bench on the landing, dropping onto it like his spirit had been plumb sucked right out of him—a phenomenon he'd seen before in older clients, his own grandparents. As somebody who wasn't crazy about people telling him what to do, either, he empathized with the old man a lot more than he might've expected.

"So what's this all gonna cost me?"

Noah walked over to crouch in front of him. "Until I run the figures, I can't give you an exact estimate. But to be honest, it's not gonna be cheap." When Charley's mouth pulled down at the corners, Noah laid a hand on his forearm. "Tell you what—how about I prioritize what should be done first, and what can maybe wait for a bit? Your niece is right, a lot of this really shouldn't be put off much longer. But nobody's trying to push you into doing anything you're not ready to do. Right, Roxie?"

When he looked at her, though, she had the oddest expression on her face. Not scared, exactly, but…shook up. Like she'd seen a ghost. At her uncle's, "What do you think, Rox?" she forced her gaze from Noah's to give Charley a shaky smile.

"Sounds more than fair to me."

Nodding, Charley hoisted himself to his feet again and crossed the few steps to the bathroom, while Noah tried to snag Roxie's attention again, hoping she'd give him a clue as to what was going on. No such luck.

"Mae picked out that tile when we moved in," Charley said, then gave a little laugh. "Said the pink was kind to her complexion…" He grasped the door frame, clearly trying to pull himself together. "She would've been beside herself, though, that I'd let the place slide so much, and that's the truth of it. Should've seen to at least some of it long ago. But…"

Noah came up behind him to clamp a hand on Charley's shoulder. "But change is scary, I know. Sometimes even when you want it—"

"Charley?"

Both men turned to look at Roxie, whose smile seemed a little too bright. "What's Mae saying about this?"

Charley sighed. "That I'm being a damn fool."

"And…?" Roxie prompted.

Flummoxed, Noah watched Charley tilt his head, his eyes closed for several seconds before he opened them again. "She says to tell Noah to get going on that estimate.

So I guess, since I never refused my wife anything while she was alive, no sense in starting now."

Dear Lord.

Roxie walked Noah downstairs and to the front door, her arms crossed like she was deep in thought.

"Hey. You okay?"

"What? Oh. Yes." Finally her eyes lifted to his, but almost as if she was afraid of what she'd see there. "Thank you."

"For what?"

She smiled slightly. "For blowing my preconceived notions all to hell."

Noah mulled that over for a second or two, then said, "I guess I'll get back to you in a few days, then."

"Sounds good," she said, opening the front door to a landscape a whole lot whiter than it'd been a half hour ago. Noah stopped, shoving his hands in his pockets. "I take it you humor the old man about hearing his wife?"

That got a light laugh and a shrug. "Who am I to decide what he does and doesn't hear?" Stuffing her fists in her sweatshirt's front pouch, she squinted at the snow. "Be careful, it looks pretty slippery out there."

The door closing behind him, Noah tromped down the steps, thinking the pair of them were crazy as loons, and that was the God's honest truth.

Through the leaky window, Charley watched until Noah was out of sight before turning to face his niece, up to her elbows in one of the moving boxes they'd hauled out of the garage he hadn't been able to park in since 1987. The way Mae's "collections" had clearly gotten out of hand was pretty hard to swallow. That he'd become an ornery old coot who'd hung on to his wife's stuff every bit as tenaciously as she had, just because, was even harder.

However, Noah's eyeing Roxie as if she was a new item on the menu at Chili's and he hadn't eaten in a week? That was seriously annoying him. Whether she returned his interest he couldn't tell—the girl never had been inclined to share her feelings with Charley, anyway, which he'd been more than okay with until now. But as close as he was to the boy's folks, and as much as he thought the world of Gene's and Donna's other boys, his Roxie deserved far better than Noah Garrett.

"I don't imagine I have to tell you to watch out for that one."

Seated on the brick-colored, velvet sofa—definitely Mae's doing—Roxie glanced up, the space between her brows knotted. "That one?"

"Noah."

With a dry, almost sad laugh, she shook her head and dived back into the box. "No, you certainly don't."

"Because you know he's—"

"Not my type."

"Well. Yeah. Exactly."

She straightened, a tissue paper-wrapped lump in each hand and a weird half smile on her face. Her let's-pretend-everything's-fine-okay? look. "So, nothing to worry about, right?"

Charley yanked his sleeve hems down over his knuckles, the icy draft hiking up his back reminding him how much weight he'd lost this past year. Even he knew he looked like an underfed vulture, bony and stooped and sunken-cheeked. That seriously annoyed him, too.

"Glad we're on the same page, then," he muttered, winding his way through the obstacle course into the kitchen for a cup of tea—what did he care if the color scheme was "outdated," whatever the heck that meant?—thinking maybe he should get a cat or something. Or a dog, he thought, waiting for the microwave to ding. Lot to be said for a companion who didn't talk back. Besides, he'd read somewhere that pets were good for your blood pressure.

As opposed to busybody nieces, who most likely weren't.

Dunking his twice-used tea bag in the hot water, Charley watched her from the kitchen door. He loved the girl with all this heart, he really did, but being around her made him feel as if he was constantly treading in a stew of conflicting emotions. Some days, when the loneliness nearly choked him, he was actually grateful for her company; other days her energy and pushiness made him crazed.

More than that, though, he simply didn't know what to say to her, how to ease her pain while his own was still sharp enough to scrape. That'd been Mae's job, to soothe and heal. To act as a buffer between them. Not that Rox was a moper, thank goodness, but every time he looked at her, there it was, his own hurt mirrored in eyes nearly the same weird green as Mae's. And at this point the helplessness that came with that had about rubbed his nerves raw.

Especially compounded with her being constantly on his back to clear out Mae's stuff, to "move on" with his life. As if he had someplace to go. Even as a kid, Charley had never liked being told what to do, whether it was in his best interests or not. Like now. Because, truthfully? What earthly use did he have for all of Mae's collections? Yet part of him couldn't quite let go of the idea that getting rid of it all would be like saying the past forty years had never happened.

He turned back to the counter to dump three teaspoons of sugar in his tea, a squirt of juice from the plastic lemon in the fridge. Then, the mug cupped in his hands, he meandered back into the living room, where the glass-topped coffee table was practically buried underneath probably two dozen of those anemic-looking ceramic figurines Mae'd loved so much. Things looked like ghosts, if you asked him. "What'd you say that stuff was again?"

"Lladro," Roxie said, gently setting another piece on table, next to a half dozen others. "From Spain. Mostly from the sixties and seventies." She sat back, giving him a bemused look, the spunk in those grass-colored eyes at such odds with the sadness. "Let me guess—you don't recognize them."

"Sure I do," he lied, sighing at his niece's chuckle. "I was putting in long hours at work back then, I didn't really pay much attention."

"There's probably a hundred pieces altogether."

He'd had no idea. "You're kidding?"

Her curls shivered when she shook her head. "Even though the market's pretty saturated with Lladro right now, some of the pieces could still bring a nice chunk of change from the right buyer. Mae collected some good stuff here."

"And some not so good stuff?"

She pushed a short laugh through her nose. "True. Not sure what the demand is for four decades' worth of *TV Guide* covers, or all those boxes of buttons—although some crafter might want them. Or the Happy Meal toys. But this—" She held up another unwrapped piece. "This I know. This we can sell."

Over the pang brought on by that word "sell," Charley felt a spurt of pride, too. Maybe the girl drove him bonkers, but she was damn smart. And knowledgeable, like one of those appraisers on *Antiques Roadshow,* which Charley realized he hadn't watched since Mae's passing. And for sure, Roxie's talents were wasted in some fly speck of a village in northern New Mexico. Child needed to be someplace where she could put all that education and experience to good use.

Then he could get back to living on his own, which he'd barely gotten used to when Roxie returned and tossed everything ass over teakettle.

He leaned over and picked up one of the pieces, the flawless surface smooth and cool against his hand. "Getting any messages from Mae?" Roxie asked, a smile in her voice.

Charley set the piece back down, then took a long swallow of his tea. "Do whatever you think best," he said, feeling a little piece of himself break off, like a melting iceberg.

Although the fact was, Mae had told him before she died to sell the whole shebang, put the money into an annuity. It was him who was resisting, not Mae. Who didn't really speak to him, of course. Even if he sometimes wished she did. Lord, what he'd give to hear her laughter again.

The pretense hadn't even been a conscious decision, really. Just kind of happened one day when Roxie had been bugging him about packing up Mae's clothes, and Charley, growing increasingly irritated, heard himself say, "Mae wouldn't want me to do that," and Roxie'd said, "What?" and he said, "She told me not to get rid of her things yet," and Roxie had backed right off, much to Charley's surprise.

Charley supposed it was his subconscious stumbling upon a way to make Mae the buffer again. Not that he was entirely proud of using his dead wife in this manner, but if it got Roxie off his case? Whatever worked. And that way it wasn't *him* changing his mind, it was Mae.

Long as he didn't carry things too far. Dotty was one thing, incompetent another. Fortunately the hospice social worker—who Roxie'd contacted without his say-so—had reassured her it wasn't uncommon for the surviving spouse to imagine conversations with the one who'd gone on, it was simply part of the grieving process for some people, it would eventually run its course and she shouldn't become overly concerned.

So it would. Run its course. Soon as "hearing" Mae no longer served his purpose, he'd "realize" he no longer did.

Two more pieces unwrapped and noted in that spiral notebook she carried everywhere with her, Roxie glanced up. "You okay? You're awfully quiet."

He decided not to point out he could say the same about her. And he was guessing Noah Garrett had something to do with that.

"Nothing to say, I suppose," he said as the powerless feelings once again threatened to drown him. "Need some help unwrapping?"

"Only if you want to."

He didn't. Outside, the wind picked up, the wet snow slapping against the bay window, slithering down the single-paned glass behind the flimsy plastic panels he popped into their frames every year. Simply watching the plastic "breathe" as it fought valiantly but inefficiently against the onslaught made him shiver. Roxie glanced over, then reached behind her for one of the new plush throws she'd bought at Sam's Club to replace the sorry, tattered things that had been around since the dawn of time, wordlessly handing it to him.

Charley didn't argue. Instead, he tucked it around his knees. "New windows included in that estimate Noah's gonna give us?"

Shoving a pencil into her curls, Roxie smiled. "What's Mae say about it?"

"Mae's not the one freezing her behind off," Charley snapped. "So. Am I getting new windows or not?"

Rolling her eyes, Roxie pulled her cell phone and what

Charley assumed was the shop's card out of her sweatshirt's pocket and punched in a number. While she waited for somebody to pick up, she glanced over, a tiny smile on her lips. "Mae would be very proud of you, you know."

Charley grunted—only to nearly jump out of his skin when he heard, clear as day, *You want me to be proud? Fix Roxie. Then we'll talk.*

Chapter Three

"This is still way over Charley's budget, Dad," Noah said, frowning past his oldest brother, Silas's shoulder at the computer screen as the accountant ran the figures for the third time.

"Then we'll simply have to shave off some more," his father said. Silas quietly swore, then sighed.

Even though Gene insisted they'd do the work for practically cost, no matter how much they whittled, the estimate still stubbornly hovered around twice what Charley could afford, according to the figure Noah'd finally wormed out of him when he'd gone back to shore up his figures the following day. Oh, there was enough for the repairs, to get the guy some new double panes, but the bright blue daisies had probably been given a reprieve. And Roxie was not gonna like that, boy.

Not that Noah should care. It wasn't her house, and she wasn't Noah's…anything. In fact, after that little exchange between Roxie and her uncle about hearing Mae's voice…

Yeah. *That* he would do well to remember. Also, the woman's pain-in-the-butt potential was through the roof. And did he need that in his life?

He did not.

Speaking of butts…Noah pulled his head out of his when Benito, the shop foreman, called Gene out of the office and Silas pushed away from the computer with a noisy sigh, crossing his hands behind his head. Silas's involvement in the family business was limited to number crunching and filing taxes, but since the bottom line was what made the difference between success and a whole bunch of people starving to death, his input was crucial.

And now his short dark brown hair was a mess from his repeatedly ramming his hand through it over the past hour. "And you're sure Charley wasn't lowballing *his* figure?"

"Since I'm not privy to the man's bank account, I have no idea. But he's only going to spend what he's going to spend."

One side of Silas's mouth hiked up before he removed his wire-rimmed glasses to rub his eyes. "True," he said, shoving the glasses back on. "But even if you do the absolute minimum, Dad's cutting this way too close for comfort. My comfort, at least."

Straightening, Noah crammed his hands in his back pockets, frowning at the figures on the screen as if he could will them to change. "There's really no wiggle room at all, is there?"

"Nope. Meaning he'll have to eat any cost overruns."

"Then I'll just have to make sure there aren't any."

Silas snorted, then leaned forward again, apparently unaware of the SpongeBob sticker clinging to the back of his navy sweatshirt.

"I know this is your project—"

Noah snorted.

"—but can I make a suggestion?"

"Sure."

"Let's tack on another five percent to cover our backsides, in case lumber prices go up or something. Because you know what'll happen—things'll get tight, and Dad will get stressed—"

"And Mom will be all over us about how *we* let things get out of hand. Yeah, I know. And I would've suggested it if you hadn't. Except…" He cuffed the back of his neck, glowering at the screen. Or rather, the image of Roxie's sad, mad green eyes. "Adding five percent to our price isn't going to add it to his budget."

"And sometimes," Silas said quietly, "that's not our problem."

Silas was right, Noah knew he was, but… He walked around the desk to sink onto the old, dusty futon on the other side. "I did warn Roxie this might be a bigger project than she anticipated. But she's going to be pretty disappointed." A half laugh pushed through Noah's nose. "Probably more than Charley, to tell the truth. And you know Dad, he's liable to go over there himself and do it *all* for free if we're not careful. And then we're right back where we started. Having Mom mad at him. And us."

"So basically we're screwed."

"Exactly."

Silas leaned back again, taking a swig from a can of soda as he stared thoughtfully at the screen. "I suppose I could pitch in on the weekends, maybe. We could ask Jesse, too." He grinned. "Make baby brother earn his keep for once."

Noah chuckled. "Baby" brother, in charge of the business's promotion and advertising, earned his keep fine.

However, homeboy was also built like an ox and not incompetent with a power saw.

"That might work—"

"Get Roxie in on the action herself, too. Why not?" Silas said to Noah's frozen expression. "No reason why she couldn't do a lot of the demo, whatever doesn't require a whole lot of expertise, save the crew for the stuff that matters." He flicked his index finger at the screen. "With enough sweat equity you might squeeze by. Think she'll go for that?"

Noah unlocked his face muscles enough to get out, "I have no idea."

"Well, I'm in," Silas said, oblivious to his brother's paralysis. "And I'm sure we can strong-arm Jesse. Might want to leave Eli out of it, though. Sleep deprivation and power tools are not a good mix."

His arms crossed, Noah grunted. "And you guys wonder why I'm perfectly happy leaving the kid raising to you."

"Uh-huh. And I suppose Jewel had to twist your arm to build that tree house for my boys?"

"And miss an opportunity to watch your brain explode? No damn way." And before Silas could pursue the topic, Noah stood, checking his watch. "I told Roxie I'd swing by with the estimate before lunch. You mind printing it out for me?"

"See that little printer icon right there?" Silas said, rising as well to slip on his denim jacket. "Click it and watch magic happen."

"Jerk," Noah muttered, plunking his butt behind the computer and hitting Print.

"By the way," Silas said, as the ancient gray monstrosity on the dinged metal table beside the desk wheezed to life. "Jewel and I set a date. April fifth."

This said with the slightly nauseating smirk of the head-over-heels in love. Not that Noah didn't like the eccentric little midwife who'd snagged his brother's—and his two awesome little boys'—hearts. But that left Noah the last brother standing. Alone. Meaning his mother could, and undoubtedly would, now focus all her matchmaking energies on him, bless her heart. Not.

Waiting for the printer to cough up the estimates, Noah let out an exaggerated sigh. "So you're actually going through with it?"

"You know," Silas said after a moment's silence, "maybe the idea of being 'stuck' with somebody for the rest of your life gives you the heebie-jeebies, but in case you haven't noticed, not everybody sees it that way."

"Sorry," Noah mumbled, his face warming as he turned back to the printer. Silas's first marriage had sunk like a stone, followed by his ex's death in a car crash when the boys were still babies. For so long, and whether it was right or not, Silas had felt like a failure, Noah knew. So why was he taking potshots at his brother's well-deserved happiness?

Fortunately single fatherhood had turned Silas—who God knew had taken inordinate pleasure in torturing his younger brothers when they were kids—into a model of forbearance.

"Oh, you'll get yours someday," he said, cuffing Noah lightly on the back of his skull before heading out the door.

When hell freezes over, he thought as he yanked on his own jacket and scooped up the estimate, then hotfooted it out of there before his father had a chance to check the new figures.

Or before Noah could think too hard about what he was about to ask of Roxie Ducharme.

* * *

For three days, between temping as a receptionist for the town's only family practitioner, continuing to pound the virtual pavement looking for a "real" job and the unending task of sorting through her aunt's things, Roxie had kept herself so busy she'd begun to think she'd imagined the close-to-knee-buckling jolt at the end of Noah's visit earlier in the week.

Except now he was here, his forehead creased as he gently explained to her uncle why his budget was too small by half, and there was the jolt again, stronger this time, undeniable, and she found herself nearly overcome with a sudden urge to bop the man upside the head with the kitchen towel in her hand.

Or herself.

"Well. That's that, girl," Charley said, sounding almost… disappointed. Weird. "Can't afford to do all this. So let's go with the new windows and let the rest of it ride—"

"Hold on, I'm not finished," Noah said, and Roxie's eyes flashed to his. Right there in front of her, not quite the same brown, but definitely the same kindness. The same… genuineness. That it had taken her so long to see the resemblance only proved how prejudiced she'd been. How much she'd been determined to see only what she'd wanted to see.

Her breath hitching painfully in her chest, she propelled herself out of the chair and over to the fridge to pull out stuff for lunch. Cheese. Ham. Lettuce. Leftover spaghetti sauce. Cottage cheese.

"Roxie?" she heard over the roaring inside her head. "You listening?"

Sucking in a breath, Roxie shoved the streak of wetness off her cheek and turned. Both men were frowning at her.

"I'm—" She cleared her throat. Sniffed. "Sorry."

"You okay?" Noah asked, simply being nice again, and more memories surged to the surface, memories she'd assumed the spectacular implosion with Jeff had wiped out for good.

Silly her.

"Yes, fine," she said, snatching the three-page estimate off the table and leafing through it. Forcing herself to focus. Holy moly. "I'm sorry," she repeated. "If I'd realized..." Letting the papers flutter back onto the kitchen table, she crossed her arms against the sick, you-screwed-up-again feeling roiling in the pit of her stomach. It wasn't as if Noah hadn't warned her, warned both of them, how costly the project might be. But this was...

Wow.

Roxie never begged or bargained or haggled. Ever. So even though embarrassment seared her cheeks, she said, "I d-don't suppose there's any way to, um, bring down the prices...?"

"Not without jeopardizing our payroll," Noah said, his eyes even more apologetic than his voice. "But—"

"Then...I guess we'll have to stick with the windows. And maybe the front porch—?"

He chuckled. "You weren't listening, were you?"

"Um...I thought I was—"

Charley slapped the table in front of him, making both the sugar bowl and Roxie jump. "Man says if enough people pitch in to help—you know, do some of the easier stuff— Noah and his crew can handle the rest and we might be able to get everything done for the same price."

Roxie felt her forehead pinch. "I don't understand."

"Silas offered to help since things are slow, taxwise, right now," Noah said. "Maybe Jesse, too." Noah glanced down, then back up at her with a little-boy grin. "And we figure there's a lot you could do, too. If you're amenable."

She wasn't sure what was making her heart beat faster—the grin, the eyes or the proposal. To gather her thoughts—and break the mesmeric hold Noah had on her gaze—Roxie frowned at her uncle.

"And you're okay with this?"

"Heck, yeah."

"Even though three days ago you were ready to throttle me for even thinking of changing anything in the house… oh." She sighed. "Mae?"

Her uncle's smile faltered for a second before he gave a vigorous nod. "It'll be like an old-fashioned barn raising! Or one of those HGTV shows! So whaddya say, Rox? You up for ripping off some wallpaper? Slapping on some paint?"

Roxie sighed. On the face of it, it was a brilliant plan. In some ways it could even be fun. But…working alongside Noah? Hot, sweaty, sexy, gentle-to-old-men, *major player* Noah?

Who strangely reminded her of someone who'd broken her heart ten times more than sorry-assed Jeff could even dream about?

"It won't work without you," Noah said, sounding even more reluctant about the whole idea than she. If that was possible.

Oh, boy. Part of her would rather dance naked with African bees. But as much as her uncle and she got on each other's nerves, she loved the old grouch. And she really did worry about the house falling down around his ears. So… if she sucked it up now, she could leave later with a clear conscience. Right?

Not only that, but considering what she'd put him and Mae through after her parents died? She supposed she could deal with Noah's hotness for a few weeks.

"I'd have to see what I can work out with the clinic," she said. "But sure, why not?"

Charley let out a whoop and clapped his hands, his wide grin warming her heart—even as Noah's twisted it like a wrung-out washcloth.

Family dinner nights at Noah's parents' were not for the faint of heart. Especially as his brothers' broods grew and the noise level increased exponentially. However, unless somebody's wife was giving birth or there were flu germs involved, there was no "will not be attending" option.

So here Noah slouched on the scuffed-up old leather sectional in the relatively quiet family room, his belly full of his mother's pot roast and his head full of Roxie—even though he had a date later that evening with some chick he met while working on a project in Chama—all by his lonesome. Well, except for his father's old heeler seeking refuge from way too many shrill little voices and eager little hands, and Eli's sacked-out, newborn son hunched underneath his chin.

That he was even thinking of canceling only went to show how messed up he was. Wasn't as if he'd never had more than one woman on the brain at once, for heaven's sake. Not that he'd ever two-timed anybody, exactly—he was capable of monogamy, especially once getting naked was involved, and as long as nobody was talking long-term. Except, truth be told, things went down that road a lot less often than people assumed. Having a few laughs, kicking up his heels on the dance floor, simply enjoying a pretty gal's company…that's about as far as the vast majority of his dates went. And sometimes, when things were totally casual…his mind wandered.

Or, he thought morosely as the baby squirmed and gurgled softly in his sleep—and Blue lifted his head to make sure The New One was okay—got stuck someplace it shouldn't. Tonight, much to his consternation, he couldn't blast Roxie out of his head.

"Aw—don't you two look adorable?" his sister-in-law Tess whispered, still cute as all get-out despite the bags under her deep brown eyes. He supposed she and his next older brother, Eli, qualified as high school sweethearts, despite the ten years of Tess's subsequent marriage to, and two children by, someone else. But now here they were, together again and blissfully adding to the world population. Somebody shoot him now.

At the sound of his mama's voice little Brady let out a "feed me" squawk. Smiling, the brunette carefully peeled the kid and receiving blanket off Noah's shoulder. "You're such a good uncle."

"And don't you forget it," he said, telling himself he didn't miss the warmth, the slight weight. The trust. Knowing he didn't miss the responsibility at all.

No sooner had Tess left, however, than his dad came in, dropping with a satisfied groan into the brown La-Z-Boy recliner that had been around longer than Noah.

"Your mother will be the death of me one of these days," Gene said, his hands clamped over his stomach, "but damn, she can cook."

Noah regarded his father for a moment, thinking about how tangled his and his father's relationship was, that they could be so close and yet butt heads so often. And so hard. "I take it your stomach's okay then?"

"What? Oh. Yeah, yeah, fine. Couldn't be better."

"Glad to hear it," Noah said, leaning forward to push himself off the sofa. But his father's hand shot out.

"Hang on a minute, I want to talk to you." Grunting, he curled over the arm of the chair to dig the remote out of the pocket. The clicker found, he aimed it at the flat-screen TV, talking to the screen instead of Noah. "Why'd you jack up the figures for Charley's job?"

Sneaking a glance at his watch—it was too late to cancel now without looking like a sleazeball—Noah lowered himself again to the edge of the sofa, his hands linked between his knees. "Because you'd cut them too close," he said over some crime show he never watched. "If any of our supply prices had gone up, you'd've been screwed. And Silas agreed with me," he added before his father could protest.

"Damn repeats," his father muttered, clicking the TV off again before meeting Noah's gaze. "Except Charley doesn't have that kind of money."

"I understand that. Since I was the one who discussed the budget with him. So we all came up with a solution."

"We all?"

"Silas and me, mostly. But Roxie, too. That if a lot of the demo work got done for free, Charley's contribution would still cover materials and the crew's wages. There's like zip profit margin, but it won't take you under, either."

His father looked at him steadily for several seconds. "What about your salary?"

"I'm good for a couple of weeks. Shouldn't take any longer than that."

More staring. "Why?"

Noah knew what he was asking. "Because I know how much Charley means to you."

His father broke the connection first, shifting in his chair and turning the TV back on. "Roxie know you're doing the project gratis?"

"No. Why should she?"

The uncomfortable silence that followed was broken by Donna Garrett's hearty laugh from the dining room, where she was supervising dessert for a batch of grandchildren. "Guess that could work."

Noah knew the grudging acknowledgement was as close to a thumbs-up as Gene was going to give under the circumstances. Before he could reply, however, his father said, "I've been thinking about what you said. About how I should spend some time with your mother." He drummed his fingers on the arm of the chair. "Get away."

"Oh?"

"Except…what if I did want to go traipsing around Europe or take your mother on a cruise or something? Who'd handle things while I was gone?"

And here we go again. "Actually…probably the same people who handle things now." When his father frowned at him, Noah said, "Dad. Everybody knows you worked your butt off all those years when we were little. And that the business wouldn't be what it is today if you hadn't. But it also wouldn't be what it is if it wasn't for all of us. You gotta admit, you haven't run it on your own for some time." And it occurred to Noah that he wasn't asking for a go-ahead to take on more responsibility as much as an acknowledgement that he, and his brothers, already had.

Gene met his gaze dead on. "You telling me I'm no longer necessary?"

"Didn't say that. But it's been a long time since you were the sole decision maker—"

"Maybe so. But you all, you're…" His father made a circle with one hand, like he was searching for the right word. "Spokes of the same wheel. And a wheel's nothing without an axle."

Smiling slightly, Noah got to his feet, checking to be sure his phone was in his jeans pocket before grabbing his jacket off the seat beside him. "Axle's kind of pointless without the wheel, too, you know. This family, it's a team. We got the whole working-together-for-the-common-good thing down. Nobody's trying to put you out to pasture, okay? But I think, between us, we can keep things going for a couple of weeks while you take Mom on a second honeymoon."

"The cabinetry, though—that's still the core of the business. The biggest moneymaker. Who's gonna oversee that?"

Noah felt his good humor quickly fade. "Me. Who else?"

His father looked away. "I don't know, Noah…."

"Okay, Dad, that's it." At Gene's startled expression, Noah hauled in a breath. "Maybe it's your prerogative that you don't agree with how I live my life. Although I would think, since I've never shown up drunk or stoned, or messed up a job, that would count for something. But whatever."

He shrugged into his jacket. "But it really chaps my hide that you apparently don't believe I'm every bit as dedicated to this business as you are. That I know it inside out. Probably better than you do at this point, since I'm the one keeping up with the technological advances and what all. I love you and I respect you, but it sure would be nice to see that respect returned, you know?

"Now if you'll excuse me, I've got a date. And no, you don't know her and probably never will, and maybe that makes me a flawed human being in your eyes." Shoving his hands in his jacket pockets, he softly said, "But that doesn't mean you can't count on me not to screw up what's really important."

His father and he did the gaze-wrestling thing for several seconds before, sighing, Noah walked away.

Chapter Four

Jumping at the duck's quacking a foot from his head, Noah grabbed for his phone off the nightstand, his brain coughing up *Who the hell changed my ring tone?* long before his bleary eyes made out the teeny, tiny numbers of the display. When he did, he jumped again, nearly dropping the phone trying to get it to his ear.

"Ma—?"

"What on earth did you say to your father last night? He's gone all mopey and won't tell me why."

Noah crashed back into his pillows, willing his heart to settle back down as he registered it was still dark. On a Saturday. "I take it you know it's not even seven yet?" he said, his eyes finally adjusting to the murky light in the bedroom. "And why are you automatically assuming I had anything to do with—?"

"Noah. Please. So what went down between the two of you?"

"I don't suppose this could wait?"

"No, it can't."

Blowing out a silent breath, Noah shoved back his black-and-tan comforter—chosen by sheer virtue of not looking like something out of either a palace or a brothel—and swung his legs over the edge to hook his abandoned jeans with one foot and kick them into his hand.

"Same old same old," he muttered around a yawn as he yanked them up one-handed, then lurched to the kitchen of his over-the-garage apartment—on the other side of town from his parents—to punch on the coffeemaker. Donna Garrett was well aware of the ongoing conflict between him and his father, no need to rehash the whole thing. Especially before coffee. "Except this time I might've put my foot down a little more. For his sake. And yours."

"Mine?"

"Yeah," Noah said, kicking on the thermostat. Dang, it was cold. "Because he told me you've been after him to take some time off. Since I agree—" although even he knew better than to bring up the Tums episode "—I had to convince him the business wouldn't fall apart if he left for a few weeks. Why are you laughing?"

"You know, sometimes I really wonder how your father and I have made it through all these years without killing each other."

"That's easy." Noah yawned again and forced his eyes open a little wider. "Neither one of you wanted to be left raising us on your own."

She laughed again. "You got that right. But the thing is…he did ask me if I wanted to get away, maybe after Christmas. A cruise."

Noah stopped in the middle of scratching his stubbled cheek. "You serious?"

"I am. And apparently he is, too. Except he practically

growled the suggestion. Didn't exactly make me want to hop online to search for cruise clothes. Now, though, things are making more sense." She laughed again, more softly. "He *listened* to you, Noah. Whatever issues the two of you might have, he listened. So thank you, honey. From the bottom of my heart."

The coffee ready, Noah filled a mug already sitting on the counter, wincing when a single, grudging shaft of light pierced the kitchen blinds. The first hit of caffeine sent off to swim through his veins, he said, "It doesn't bother you that it wasn't Dad's idea?"

"Are you kidding? If left to his own devices, the man would be perfectly content going to work, coming home, eating, watching TV and sleeping. Rinse, repeat. With maturity comes the ability to be grateful for the *what,* and not worry so much about the *how.* You might have annoyed him no end, but in one conversation you pushed him further out of his comfort zone than I've been able to do in twenty years."

She rang off after that, about ten seconds before Noah's bladder exploded and a good two, three minutes before the ramifications of his father's actions sank in: that maybe, finally, Noah'd gotten through to the old man. That maybe, finally, he'd earned the old man's trust.

A smile spreading across his face, he yanked up the blinds to let in more light. His date last night had gone better than expected—enough that the prospect of meeting Roxie at Lowe's later to hash out tile and paint selection and such wasn't even bothering him—and his father *trusted* him.

Was this going to be a great day, or what?

"What the hell do I know about any of this?" Charley barked. Loudly enough to make everybody in the tile aisle turn their heads. Roxie was briefly tempted to say, "I have

no idea who this guy is, never saw him before in my life."
Instead, she lugged a large square of veined slate tile off
the sale pile and held it up. "This would go great with the
new countertops, don't you think?"

Her uncle grunted, as cranky as a three-year-old who'd
missed his nap. In theory, a field trip to Santa Fe to choose
the decorative materials for the renovation had sounded like
the perfect thing for a beautiful fall morning. In reality…
not so much.

"Whatever you pick out is fine," Charley muttered. "I
don't care. Actually, why don't I go wait in the car until
you're finished?"

Replacing the tile before it somehow found itself shat-
tered over the old man's head, Roxie sighed. "Charley. It's
your house. Where you're going to be living for a long,
long time. I'd think you'd want to be in on the decision
making."

His face set in a mulish expression, her uncle shoved
his hands in his baggy khaki pockets. At least they were
an improvement over the god-awful coveralls. He'd been
a good-looking dude once upon a time, when he actually
took pride in his appearance.

"And why would you think that? Never did when Mae
was alive, still not interested now."

Roxie opened her mouth to make him see reason, only
to realize at this rate they'd be here until Christmas. Ten
years from now.

"If you really don't care—"

Charley's eyes snapped to hers, full of hope. "I really
don't."

"Fine. Why don't you wait in that Burger King we saw
when I parked the car? I'll meet you there when I'm done.
But no complaints about whatever I choose!" she called to
his rapidly retreating form as she fished her ringing cell

phone from her purse. Noah. She told herself the funny, fluttering sensation in her midsection was a hunger pang.

"Just walked through the door," he said, damn his bone-melting voice. "Where are you?"

"Tile. I think I found something that could work."

"Cool. Um…is that Charley headed out the exit?"

"Yep. I thought he'd like to be involved. I was wrong…." She looked up to see Noah turn into the aisle—all wind-blown and hunky and competent-looking—and she felt another "hunger" pang.

She dropped her phone back into her purse, pointing to the tile as Noah drew close enough for her to catch a whiff of wood-smoke-and-leather-scented stud. This time it wasn't her stomach growling. "What do you think?" she said, trying not to breathe.

He hefted a square in his hand, turned it over to give it an approving look. Hormones surged. "Good stuff," he said. "Especially at this price."

"Oh. Great."

He looked at her funny. "You have a cold?"

"What? Oh. No. I'm, um…it's the lumber smell, I guess. Tickles my nose. Anyway…so that tile for the floor. And maybe this—" she scooted down the aisle to a display of netted, one-inch tiles in coordinating shades of beige "—for the backsplash?"

"Excellent," Noah said. Grinning. But not at her, she surmised. Let alone about her.

"You seem awfully chipper this morning."

The grin broadened. "I suppose I am."

When no explanation followed—not that Roxie needed, or even wanted, one—she said, "Well. Anyway. Here's the paint samples, but I don't know how much to get—"

"Don't worry about that," he said, flipping through the samples, which she'd already marked for each room. "I'll pick it up, use my discount. So those tiles, and these, and you chose the laminate for the counter. Wanna see those tub surrounds I told you about?"

So they did, and she approved, and then they discussed schedules and things, and it was all very businesslike and professional, and little by little Roxie found herself actually becoming more impressed with Noah's expertise than his scent.

Hope. Yay.

Noah knew all about the theory that men's brains couldn't multitask, especially when anything even vaguely resembling sex was involved. *Well, screw that,* he thought, as they walked toward the parking lot after submitting his purchase orders at the customer service desk. Because the whole time he'd done the professional contractor act with Roxie, another part of his brain kept firing off random, totally unprofessional observations.

Like how the overhead lighting made her curls all shiny.

That her top blouse button underneath her corduroy jacket stopped just short of showing any cleavage.

The way the space between her dark, natural eyebrows would pucker in concentration when he explained something, even when she was smiling.

That he was already having trouble remembering what's-hertootsies from last night. Although the restaurant had been kick-ass.

"By the way," Roxie said, "I worked out my schedule with the clinic. Since Naomi's usually busier in the afternoons and evenings, anyway, I can work on the house every morning and one full day during the week. How's that?"

Huddled inside her jacket from the brisk breeze, she squinted up at him. She wasn't particularly short—sort of average, in fact—but he was tall enough for there to be an appreciable difference. A stray curl drifted across her eyes; she shoved it behind her ear, studded with a single, small gold loop. If he looked closely he could see a bunch of tiny dots from other, closed-up piercings. Funny, how he'd never even really noticed Goth Roxie, and yet he couldn't take his eyes off Real Roxie.

"Sounds good," he said. "How early you want to start?"

"I'm usually up by six. So whenever."

"I'm not, so…eight?"

She laughed. The kind of laugh that made you want to laugh back. The curl blew into her face again, but this time she let it go. "Eight's fine," she said, even as Noah decided that curl would be the undoing of him. Seriously.

He glanced out into the parking lot. "Where you parked?"

"Over there," she said, pointing. "But I have to fetch Charley first. I banished him to Burger King. Anyway," she said, turning and walking backward, her teeth chattering. "So…I'll see you Monday?"

"Actually, I could go for a hamburger myself," he said, falling into step beside her, even though the rational part of his brain screamed, *Run, fool! Run!* "If it's all the same to you."

"Suit yourself," she said, clutching her jacket collar underneath the chin.

"You're freezing."

"Wh-what w-was your f-first cl-clue?"

"Here," Noah said, placing a hand on her waist to gently shift her over. "Walk on this side, it's not as windy next to the buildings."

"Oh. Um. Yeah, you're right." Her eyes flitted to his. "Thanks."

"Anytime. That your phone?"

"What? Oh…damn," she said, digging it out of her purse. "I can never hear it when I'm outside. But let me forget to turn it off at the movies, and it sounds like a symphony… orchestra.…"

As her voice faded, Noah looked over. She was still walking, but kind of like a robot. "You gonna answer it?"

"No," she said, stuffing it back into the bag as they reached the Burger King, the warm, intoxicating scent of fast food enveloping them when Noah opened the door.

"What the heck?" Roxie muttered beside him; frowning, Noah followed her gaze…to a table in the back, where Charley sat with a red-headed Shirley MacLaine look-alike, looking a lot more interested in her than his burger.

"I swear, I was just sitting there, minding my own business, and up comes this gal, asking if the seat was taken." Charley traipsed over to the soon-to-be-history kitchen cupboard to get the box of tea bags—but with a spring in his step that reminded Roxie an awful lot of Noah. Dear God.

Her name was Eve. No, Eden. Dyed red hair, lots of jewelry. And makeup, not badly applied. Perfume, however, strong enough to overpower the fast-food fumes. Hailed from New Jersey, lived in Santa Fe for ten years. Had immediately assumed Noah and Roxie were a couple. Not that that stopped her from flirting with him, Roxie'd noticed.

"And what's up with the attitude, anyway?" Charley said. "Thought you were so hot for me to move on?"

"Charley," Roxie said over the ten kinds of alarms going off inside her head. "You just met the woman—"

"We hit it off. Go figure. So I'm taking her to the movies tomorrow night. But could I borrow your car? The Blue Bomb's not the sort of vehicle you take a gal out in.

Especially for a first date. And get this—she's crazy about action movies." Charley laughed, the sound freer than Roxie'd heard since her aunt's death. More alarms went off. At this rate, she'd be deaf before nightfall. "In fact, you should've seen the look on her face when I suggested that new Meryl Streep flick. Like she'd swallowed something nasty."

Oh, dear. Poor guy had it bad.

"Maybe…you shouldn't rush into anything."

Dunking his tea bag in the mug of hot water, her uncle shot her a reproving look from underneath his eyebrows. "I'd hardly call a movie date *rushing*. And since when are you my mother?"

"Since you started picking up chicks in Burger King?"

"Not sure which bugs me more," he said, leaning against the counter on the other side of the room. "That you don't think I'm smart enough to spot a gold digger—"

"I never said—"

"Or that I deserve to have a little fun."

"Of course I want you to have some fun! A lot of fun! As much fun as you like! It's just…"

"You think this is a rebound."

"I think I should check for the empty love potion bottle. This zero-to-sixty business is a little unnerving." When he shot her another mulish look—albeit of a much spunkier variety than the one he'd given her in the tile aisle—she said, "Charley, I know how down you've been since Mae's death, which wasn't all that long ago—"

"More than a year, Rox. And at my age, there are worse things than a rebound relationship." He shrugged. "Should it even come to that." Then his eyes found hers. "This isn't the same situation as yours, because I'm not looking for the same things. At this point, whatever happens from now on…" Another shrug. "Gravy."

One arm across her ribs, Roxie ducked her head to stare at a mystery splotch on the disgusting floor. "Maybe you're not in the same place I was…back then. But still. Acting on an attraction when you're still in love with someone else—"

"It's a *date,* Rox. That's all. Now can we drop this?"

"No. The dating scene…it's changed since you dated Mae. A lot."

"And you think I'd have a *problem* with having sex on the third date?" At her apparently appalled expression, Charley chuckled. "Your aunt and I got cozy on the second. Betcha didn't expect that, didja?"

"Geez, Charley—"

"It was the sixties. What can I say? Sex happened."

"This is supposed to be reassuring?"

"Although," he said on a sigh, "now that *I'm* in my sixties, sex probably isn't going to happen quite so much. Listen, you don't think I'm shocked, too? That one minute, I'm a lonely old man, the next, here's this pretty woman, asking if she can sit with me, and suddenly we're talking like we've known each other forever. Her dead husband, he also worked at Los Alamos. Although in a completely different department. And get this—"

"She was a teacher, too?"

"Yeah. How'd you know? Only she taught little kids, first grade. Not high school. So can I borrow your car tomorrow?"

Roxie had to admit, as the initial shock began to fade, Charley excited about going on a date with someone he barely knew was far preferable to Charley still mourning someone he'd known and loved his entire adult life. And of course he was perfectly capable of looking out for himself. No point putting her own issues on the poor man.

"Yes, Charley. You can borrow the car." Her mouth

twitched. "But put gas in it. And if you're not home by midnight your car privileges are revoked."

"No problem, we're going to the afternoon show, it's cheaper that way. So how'd you and Noah get on with the selections?"

And, apparently, that was the end to that conversation.

Her issues, no. The conversation, yes.

"Fine," she said, which was the end of *that* conversation. After Charley bustled off—she assumed to confirm plans with his new "friend"—Roxie returned to the dining room to continue her unpacking, cataloguing, repacking, since everything had to be shoved back into the garage until after the reno. The better pieces she'd decided to sell on eBay, but she'd have to hold a yard sale or something for the rest of it. Although, between their being out in the boonies and winter breathing down their necks, how she was going to pull that off she had no idea.

That, however, was a worry for another day. Because today she had worries enough, between her uncle's finding love over a Whopper and fries and her insane attraction to Noah and her near heart attack when she'd seen Jeff's number on her cell phone earlier.

What on earth he wanted to say, she couldn't imagine. Certainly she had nothing to say to him. However, since he hadn't left a voice mail, she assumed it wasn't urgent. Or even important. And unless and until he did, she saw no reason to answer. Ever. Maybe he no longer had the power to hurt her—a power Roxie willingly admitted she'd given him—but allowing him renewed access to her head? So not happening.

A realization that only strengthened her resolve not to let Noah get to her, either, to not read his chivalrously moving her out of the wind, or his gracious reaction to Eden's erroneous assumption about them, as anything more than the actions of a man whose mama had brought him up right. Because she'd made the mistake before, of looking at someone through cloudy lenses, convincing herself the blurred image was what she wanted it to be, rather than what it was. Maybe, in Charley's case, that didn't matter.

But in hers? Yeah. It mattered.

Big time.

Noah had to hand it to Roxie—the woman's work ethic made him feel like a lazy slug.

Every morning for the past week, she'd already been at it for hours before he and the crew arrived at eight, stripping wallpaper or prepping walls or knocking out tiles. There was also always coffee brewing—she'd borrowed the giant pot from church—and some sort of baked goodies, usually courtesy of Silas's fiancée, Jewel, or his mother, since Roxie admitted cooking was not one of her talents. A comment which provoked a deep blush on her part, and a big grin on Noah's, right before she skittered away to her next project like one of Cinderella's little helpers.

Today, however, while the window dudes were putting in the new double panes, it was time to take a sledgehammer to the gouged, grungy kitchen floor tiles—she'd been sorely disappointed to discover they'd simply remove the cabinets, not pulverize them—a task Noah'd forbidden her to tackle when he wasn't there. He'd thought it a simple request; she, alas, saw it as his not trusting her to have at least *some* common sense, which in turn got his back up about her stubbornness, fueling a heated "discussion" that had left them both hot and panting, and, at least in Noah's case, turned on.

Yeah, the crew found that *very* entertaining.

Now, considering the gusto with which she pummeled the poor tiles, it didn't take a rocket scientist to figure out she was using it as therapy. Or imagining that the cheap ceramic she was crushing into smithereens was him. Just a guess.

"Hey, take it easy, or you're gonna be real sore tomorrow."

"Not an issue," came through the dust mask. And who knew safety goggles could be so sexy? *Wham!* "I lift weights." *Wham!* "And play tennis."

That explained a lot. "You lift weights?"

"Not barbells or anything, but when I was in middle school?" *Wham!* "We were doing gymnastics and my upper body strength was so lame I couldn't support myself on the parallel bars, so I decided to do something about it." *Wham!*

Giving him a whole new reason to be afraid of the woman, Noah thought as he raked the broken tile pieces into a pile. Gal could take him *down*. "You're not one for letting things simply happen, are you?"

Breathing heavily—God, he wished she'd stop that—she turned, swiping the back of her hand across her glistening forehead. Despite the frigid temperature, she'd removed her sweatshirt, revealing a baby blue T-shirt hugging a flat stomach, and breasts that, what they lacked in size, they made up for in charm. Especially with the heavy breathing thing.

She pushed down the mask. "What are you talking about?"

"I think it's safe to say you were a lot more motivated than your average twelve-year-old."

He thought he caught a glimpse of a smile. And her butt, when she turned back around. Covered in dusty denim, but whatever. Replacing the mask, she said, "I've never been your average anything."

Yeah, he was beginning to see that. And it wasn't making this attraction thing any easier.

"So where's Charley?"

At that, she grunted. "With his new lady love, I presume."

"That gal we met the other day?"

"The very one."

"I take it you're not exactly cool with this development?"

Her gaze flicked to his before—the sledgehammer propped against the broom closet—she navigated the loose tile floes to get to the coffeemaker and refill a mug the size of the Indian Ocean. In went an untold number of fake sugar packets and a healthy dose of half-and-half; then, stirring, she turned to lean against the counter.

"They've seen each other every day this week. And I know I should be happy for him, that he's found someone to take his mind off Mae, but…" She took a sip of coffee, then shook her head. "I can't help feeling it's too much, too fast."

Noah decided to refill his own Thermos bottle, thinking that he'd seen Charley and Roxie together enough to surmise theirs wasn't the easiest relationship, probably because they were both stubborn as mules. But if her wretched expression was any indication, she was genuinely concerned for the guy. And it got to him in ways he couldn't even define, that she cared that much. Even so…

"He is an adult, Rox," he said, his back to her as he poured.

"An adult who still hears his dead wife talk to him."

Noah turned. "So maybe Mae told him this was okay."

A frown preceded, "That doesn't bother you? That he hears dead people?"

He chose his words carefully. "Not for me to say. Long

as she's not telling him to break the law, can't see the harm in it."

A brief smile touched Roxie's mouth before she sighed again. "In any case, Mae's not here. I am. And something… just doesn't feel right. I mean, not once has Charley brought Eden here. Or suggested we all have lunch or dinner together or something—" She shook her head, one hand lifting. "Sorry, didn't mean to drag you into family business. And I've only got an hour before I have to go to the clinic, so we better get back to work, right?"

She may as well have slapped him. Noah stood there like a grade-A idiot, wanting to say…something. Anything. To plead his case…for what? The words jammed at the back of his throat, a jumbled mess he couldn't sort out to save his life.

"Yeah, whatever you say," he mumbled, thunking his mug onto the counter and grabbing a shovel.

A few minutes later, he carted the first load of tile out to the Dumpster at the bottom of the steep driveway, taking more pleasure than usual in the deafening crash when he hurled them inside. Wasn't as if he actually *enjoyed* listening to women bitch and moan, although he'd gotten better about faking it over the years, figuring it just came with the territory. So why was her dismissal ticking him off so much now?

When he returned, she was staring at her phone, her expression exactly like it'd been that Saturday outside Lowe's. Spotting Noah, she shoved it back in her pocket, clearly distressed. Clearly not sharing.

Flat-out annoyed at this point—whether that made sense or not—Noah jerked the wheelbarrow into place and began to noisily shovel in more broken tiles, even as he said, "Everything okay?"

Using a dustpan to help, Roxie added to the pile in the

wheelbarrow. "Nothing I can't handle," she said, not looking at him, and Noah felt as if his gut had caught fire.

Wasn't until the third trip down the driveway that it finally hit him that he felt exactly like he had when his father wrote him off—mad that Roxie didn't feel she could trust him, either. And again, it was nuts that he should care. Was it just the challenge of "getting" something he couldn't have? Some misguided macho sense of entitlement?

Was he really as bad as all that?

He looked back up at the house, the fear swamping him all over again, that this gal was making him feel things no other woman had ever made him feel—although at the moment, mostly like a scumbag. And suddenly nothing else mattered except gaining her trust. Even though…

Even though there was no reason on earth he deserved it.

It had already been dark for an hour when Naomi Johnson stuck her neatly dreadlocked head out of her office door and scanned the empty waiting room.

"We're done?"

"We are *done*," Roxie said, plopping the plastic cover over the printer and turning off the computer. Although, truth be told, the constant stream of patients—most of whom were under ten years old—had provided a welcome distraction from all the junk piling up in her brain. Even if seeing all those mamas with their little ones only threatened to add to the clutter, she thought, as she stood for the first time in an hour and her lower back let out a silent scream.

"You okay?" the doctor said, flicking off the office lights, leaving the waiting room bathed in a ghostly glow from the reception desk light.

"Nothing a hot bath won't cure." A wince popped out

when Roxie bent to retrieve her purse from the desk's bottom drawer. "And a dude named Sven who gets his jollies from pummeling ladies' backs. Word to the wise—sledgehammers are heavy suckers—"

"Not talking about your back, baby." Naomi paused, then said softly, "How's the job search going?"

"Oh, trust me, you'll be the first to know if anything happens on that front. Why?" Roxie said, smiling. "You anxious to get rid of me?"

"Not hardly. In fact—being purely selfish, here—I dread the day when you tell me you're leaving. Even though I know you will someday, because you've got way bigger fish to fry than temping behind a reception desk. But…" The doctor's eyes narrowed. "That's not it, either, is it?"

When Roxie looked over, the words "I'm fine" ready to jump out of her mouth, Naomi raised one graying eyebrow over her rimless glasses. Roxie sighed. At least Noah—and the confused, almost hurt look in his eyes—would be gone by the time she got back to the house. One less thing to fret about. But if her uncle *wasn't* there, she'd worry. Then again, if he was, she'd have to listen to "Eden said this" and "Eden said that" the rest of the evening. Gack.

And then there was Jeff.

"Just lots of stuff going on," she finally mumbled, yanking her jacket out of the closet and giving her back something else to screech about. At Naomi's pointed silence, she figured she might pick through the many bones and toss her one. "My ex keeps calling me," she said, because she didn't have the energy to discuss the Charley stuff, and she didn't understand the Noah stuff enough to talk about it with anybody.

"I see. And saying what?"

"Nothing, actually. Since I haven't answered the phone." Her heavy sweater slipped on over her standard office attire of jeans and a baggy sweater, Naomi frowned. "Not like you to be chicken."

"Goes to show how little you know me," Roxie said with a wan smile. "And anyway, he hasn't left a message, either, so how important could it be?"

"You forgiven him yet?"

In a rare, weak moment, shortly after Roxie started working for the doctor, Roxie had told her the details behind the breakup. Because God knows she couldn't tell Charley, and having made the mistake of making her life all Jeff, all the time, she didn't even have a girlfriend to talk to. Which naturally led to her thinking about that aborted conversation with Noah earlier in the day, halted not because she didn't want to confide in him, but because she did.

And how much sense did that make?

Realizing she hadn't answered her boss, Roxie wrapped her lacy scarf around her neck and headed toward the door, and the bracing night air beyond it, which she fervently hoped would clear her addled brain.

"I think so," she finally said, after they were both outside the pseudo Territorial-style, flat-roofed building clinging to Tierra Rosa's outskirts. In the weak circle of light from the single lamp by the door, her breath puffed white in the rapidly dropping temperature.

"Meaning?" Naomi carefully prodded.

"Meaning, once I finally accepted I was with Jeff for the wrong reasons, I found my peace. Enough peace, anyway. Not that what he did was right, but after a lot of soul-searching I realized there were things I'd refused to see. That the breakup ultimately was as much my fault as his."

Her brow furrowed, Naomi reached for Roxie's ungloved hand. "Be careful where you go with that, honey. It's one thing to own up to our mistakes. Another thing entirely to own somebody else's."

Smiling, Roxie squeezed Naomi's hand, then let go to hug herself. "I'm not doing that, I promise."

"So he really can't make you unhappy anymore?"

"Nope," she said after a moment's contemplation. "He really can't."

"Then why aren't you answering his calls?"

"Because I have nothing to say to him?"

"I understand that. But maybe he has something to say to you. And maybe, if you let him do that, you'll find the rest of your peace. Just a thought," Naomi said, turning toward her SUV, parked at the other end of the small lot. Then she pivoted back. "You know you can call me, right? If you want someone to talk to, whatever. Since heaven knows my own girls don't need me anymore," she said with the laugh of a proud mom whose grown kids were doing pretty darn well for themselves, thank you.

"I know," Roxie said, even though she probably never would. "Night."

After Naomi drove off, Roxie leaned against the hood of her middle-aged Prius, staring up into the navy sky, dotted with a billion benignly twinkling stars. Even after all these months of being away from the city, it was hard to wrap her head around the absolute stillness out here, save for the whispering of a nearby stand of pines, the distant yap-yap-yap of somebody's dog—

Her phone rang; her stomach jumped. Not Jeff, though—Noah. Not exactly better.

"Everything okay?" she said, climbing behind the wheel.

"Depends on how you define that." He paused. "But thought you'd like some warning."

Her stomach fisted again. "About…?"

Noah lowered his voice. "I was about to finish up here when your uncle arrived. With Eden."

"O-oh?"

"And enough pizza for an army. Figured you probably didn't want to walk into that unprepared."

"Depends on what kind of pizza it is," she muttered, then pushed out a breath. "Thanks—"

"And Eden insisted I stay."

Roxie closed her eyes. "I see."

"Hey. If it'd been up to me, I'd've begged off, but far be it from me to break the poor gal's heart. Besides, I'll be doing you a favor. By sticking around."

"And...how is that?"

"Trust me. You do not want to face the pair of them alone."

"Bad?"

"Times ten."

Grrreeeaaaat. Her back tensing even more, Roxie drummed her fingertips on the wheel, considering her options. Which all sucked.

"I'll be there in five minutes," she said wearily as she put the car into gear, so, *so* wishing she could rewind her life to, like, the beginning.

Chapter Five

Unfortunately, Noah had not been exaggerating.

Not that Roxie had anything against bright colors, she thought as she nibbled at a mozzarella-draped mushroom across the dining room table from the happy couple. Or jewelry. Or belly laughs. Or even, in theory, crazy older ladies, who generally seemed happy enough in their own little worlds.

Except Eden Fiorelli was no sweet, dotty thing who talked to her ten cats and imagined herself the heroine of an Agatha Christie novel. *The Real Housewives of New Jersey,* maybe. If there was, you know, a postmenopausal edition.

Bad Roxie, bad, she thought, almost tilting her head in an attempt to see what her uncle saw. And heard. Because who was she to judge?

"So Charley tells me," Noah said, sitting at right angles to Roxie at the table, "you used to be on Broadway?"

"Ohmigod, a million years ago," Eden said with a blush—Roxie thought, hard to tell underneath all the makeup—and a quick hitch of her low-cut blouse. "But yeah, I was a gypsy. In the chorus," she said in explanation to whoever might not know the term. "Until I married Sal when I was twenty-one. Can you imagine? God, I was a *baby*."

Then Roxie jumped when Eden, waving her half-eaten piece of pizza, spontaneously burst into some show number in a gutsy contralto that wouldn't have been half bad in, say, a football stadium. Noah tried to hide his grin. Sooo glad he was getting a kick out of this. Which was exactly what he was going to get if he didn't stop encouraging the woman.

Honestly, Roxie didn't know whether to laugh or cry. Whether to be grateful for Noah's presence or mad at herself for being glad he was there. To be pleased for her uncle—he certainly seemed to be having a blast, go figure—or worried that he was in way over his head.

Because Eden couldn't have been more different from Mae if she'd been from another galaxy.

The impromptu performance over—followed by applause from both males—Eden grinned at Roxie, her arm possessively linked around Charley's, her generous, albeit wrinkled, bosom so close to the man's face Roxie could tell he was seriously thinking of laying his cheek on it.

"You must think we're crazy, huh?" she said with a throaty chuckle, then planted a big kiss on said cheek without waiting for Roxie's reply. Another laugh preceded her taking a hot pink-tipped finger to the lipstick smudge. "Good thing your wife's not around," she said, "or we'd both be in *big* trouble."

Roxie nearly choked on her pepperoni—partly due to Eden's remark, partly to her uncle's guffaw in response and partly due to Noah's briefly squeezing her knee underneath the table. Her eyeballs were having an existential crisis, not knowing who to gape at first. What the hell was *wrong* with everybody?

Eden grabbed another piece of pizza—the woman definitely did not eat like a bird—her mirror-spangled angel sleeve about to drag in the sauce.

"Oh! Your sleeve—"

Another laugh as she jerked the sleeve to safety. "Thanks, doll! I am such a slob, it's ridiculous. So whaddya think of this fabric, isn't it *gorgeous?* And I'll let you in on a secret—" the bosoms puddled on the table when she leaned forward "—it's a *drapery* remnant!"

"Oh. That's…amazing."

"I know, right? I got it for dirt cheap two, three years ago. I make all my own clothes, did Charley tell you? You should see my itty-bitty apartment, it's like the size of this room, right, Charley? One whole side of the living room—" dramatic sweep "—is nothing but shelves for my sewing and crafts and sh—stuff. Swear to God, Diva and I barely have room to *think* in there."

"Diva?"

"My Chihuahua. Sal gave her to me when we first moved out here. To help get me used to being in New Mexico, he said."

Out of the corner of her eye, Roxie saw Noah's shoulders shaking with silent laughter. Creep.

Then he cleared his throat. "So your place is small?"

"Like a postage stamp," Charley said, apparently emerging enough from his besottedness to comment. Which got a shrug from his beloved.

"Yeah," Eden said. "Couldn't afford anything bigger after Sal passed away."

Uh—boy. "When was this?"

"A year ago," Charley put in, his gaze suddenly sharp. Challenging.

"Sorry to hear that," Noah said.

"It's okay, he'd been sick a long time," Eden said, her gaze tangling with Charley's for a long, borderline-embarrassing moment before he entwined his fingers with hers. Her eyes returned to Roxie's. "It was hard, but you gotta move on, right?"

Another pointed look from her uncle. Nothing like being hoisted on your own petard.

"Of course—"

"I'm really glad to hear you say that, since, you know—" Eden grinned at Charley. Again. "—we're gettin' kinda serious and all."

"Serious?" Roxie directed to her uncle as Noah's hand landed on her knee again. Somehow, this time, she didn't mind. "You've known each other a week!"

Charley's shoulders bumped. "And a half." At *her* pointed look, he said, sounding an awful lot like the bosomy broad beside him, "Hey. This was your idea, after all."

"*My* idea—?"

"Okay," Eden said, clearly sensing she'd gone too far. "Maybe 'serious' isn't the right word—"

"It's *exactly* the right word," Charley said, looping an arm around Eden's drapery-shirred shoulder and again lancing Roxie with his gaze, a move which definitely got him an adoring look from the redhead. Loosely interpreted though that may have been.

Then Eden tore her eyes away from Charley to face Roxie. "Maybe this isn't what you had in mind for your uncle. Rather, *I'm* not exactly what you had in mind. But us Jersey girls, we learn early how to go after what we want."

Breathe, girl. Breathe. "And why, exactly," she said evenly, "do you *want* my uncle?"

"This a trick question?" Her dyed brows lifted, Eden seemed genuinely surprised. "Only because he's the sweetest thing going!"

"And I'm alive," Charley said with a shrug.

"Okay, that too," Eden added with another booming laugh. Then, to Roxie, "Hey, if you're not gonna eat your crust, can I have it?"

Unable to shake the sensation of tumbling head-over-heels down a steep hill, Roxie got to her feet and headed toward the kitchen, muttering, "Go right ahead, take whatever you want—"

"Where are you going?" Charley said with a steely note to his voice.

"I'm...done," she said, wishing more than anything she could shake off either the small-mindedness or protectiveness—and right now, she honestly could not tell the difference—preventing her from rejoicing in what Charley clearly saw as his unbelievably good fortune.

Or maybe that's envy, cupcake—

"Yeah, so are we," Eden said, either oblivious to Roxie's discomfort or putting her former stage skills to good use. "That flick starts in forty-five minutes, we better get going." Then she swooped around the table to give her, then Noah, hugs. "This was fun! We should do it more often!"

Just kill her now.

Noah watched Roxie stomp around the dusty, wrecked kitchen, slamming things into the fridge, looking like she'd slam cabinet doors, too, if there'd been any to slam. Instead, she yanked a broom out of a doorless cupboard and stomped into the living room, where she came to a dead stop in front of the new picture window.

"The crew already cleaned up?"

"Yeah, I know," Noah said behind her. "Can't count on anybody these days."

She flicked him a glance and stomped back into the kitchen, swearing when the replaced broom apparently clattered onto the floor, then returned to the living room where she dropped into a squishy floral armchair, her arms tightly crossed.

"Show's over," she said through gritted teeth. "You can leave now."

Yeah, he could. Then again, it occurred to him, if he wanted people to stop treating him like a kid, he needed to start acting like an adult. And not only when it suited his purpose.

"I'm thinking...no." When she glowered up at him, the curls a blur around her thundercloud face, Noah said, "You need to vent."

"What I need is somebody, or something, to punch."

He spread his arms. "Have at it. But you'd probably hurt your hand."

On a gurgling growl, she grabbed the throw pillow beside her; Noah braced for the slam, but all she did was strangle it to her middle.

"Although," Noah said quietly, "if you really want me to go, I will."

When several seconds passed without a response, he thought, *Fine, I tried,* then returned to the kitchen to get his jacket, nearly jumping out of his skin when he turned to find Roxie standing in the doorway.

"I don't get it. Why you're here."

"I told you. Because Eden asked me—"

"Bull. If you hadn't wanted to stay, you wouldn't've. So what's in it for you?"

Irritation spiked through him. But with himself, not her. "Cynical, much?"

Her eyes burned into his. "Damn straight. Well?"

Noah felt one side of his mouth pull up. Did this gal get his juices going, or what? "Maybe I just want you to feel like—" He gave his head a sharp shake, hoping to jar loose the right words. "Like you could talk to me. Like I'd be somebody you could talk *to*."

"Why?"

"I don't *know*, dammit. Jeebus, why do women have to analyze everything to death? Something comes to me, I either roll with it or I don't. I don't pick at it until it bleeds, for god's sake."

He thought he might have seen the hint of a smile. "You want to be my...friend?"

Uncharted territory though that might have been. Noah couldn't even remember his last platonic relationship, his brothers' wives/girlfriends excepted. And yet, if he thought about it, the idea held a certain appeal, not the least of which was—since it was obvious for many reasons nothing would ever happen between them—maybe focusing on Roxie as a *friend* would finally quash the pointless sexual attraction.

Okay, maybe that was a stretch. However...

"Believe it or not, I don't have a lot of those. Brothers, yeah. Up the wazoo. But somebody I can talk to who won't go rat me out to my mother? Not really."

Her mouth twitched. "You'd trust me that much?"

Even though the barely suppressed chuckle behind her words was at his expense, warmth spread through his chest, that he'd goosed her out of her bad mood. Even if it had been unintentional. "Yeah. I would."

She seemed to consider this for a moment before her eyes narrowed. "What about your female...companions?"

"Don't pick them for their conversational skills. And that

doesn't mean what you think," he said, actually blushing when she laughed. "It means—"

"It doesn't matter," she said, clearly enjoying the heck out of his discomfort. "Really. But I still don't understand—"

"Because I *can* talk to you," he said, the truth tumbling out of nowhere, rolling right past the fear. The absurdity. "And I *like* it. That's never happened before. No, I don't suppose we have a whole lot in common—other than fathers and uncles driving us off the deep end—but for some reason, that doesn't seem to matter. And for another thing…"

Noah swung his jacket over his shoulder, shoving his other hand in his pocket. Because, yeah, maybe there was an ulterior motive. One that dovetailed nicely with that acting like a grown-up thing. "Being totally up front here…but my dad—well, everybody, frankly—expects me to come on to you. Like I wouldn't be able to help myself, or something, just because you're hot and I'm…me. Not that it's not tempting, because you *are* hot and I *am* me, but you're not…"

He pushed out a breath. "You're not the kind of gal I usually hook up with. And obviously I'm not what you're looking for, either. But I'm getting off track here. The thing is, I know Dad loves me, but I don't think he's particularly proud of me. And if I think about it from his perspective, I can sort of understand that. I don't like it, but I'm thinking maybe some changes are in order."

Skepticism shadowed her eyes, blotting out the humor. "Really?"

"Yeah. So, I got to thinking…if I could prove I'm capable of having an actual, honest-to-God friendship with a woman, it might go a long way toward convincing Dad I don't only think with my…hormones. So—whaddya say?"

Roxie stared at Noah for a long moment, thinking, *Not that it's not tempting?*

Followed by, *You think I'm hot?*

Then, finally, his "Whaddya say?" penetrated—along with the hopeful, hopeless look in those big brown eyes—and she thought, *Hell if I know.*

"Or," she said, glad she was leaning against the door frame or she might have keeled over from the dizziness, "option number two—we could keep this completely professional—"

"Nope. Won't work."

"Because…?"

"Because I like you. And for God's sake don't ask me why. I just do. And if you think that's off-the-wall from where you're standing, you should try being inside my head right now. It's like total chaos in there."

Welcome to my world, she thought, grabbing her own jacket from where she'd dumped it over the kitchen stool and shrugging into it before tugging open the back door.

"Going somewhere?"

"Fresh air helps me think," she said, fishing her scarf from her pocket and winding it twice around her neck. And God knew she needed all the help she could get right now.

"It's cold out there."

"Sure is." She started through the door, knowing Noah would follow. Which could lead to all sorts of giddy, silly feelings, if she were inclined toward such things.

The back door actually opened up to the side yard and a walk meandering around to the Machu Pichu-esque steps between the front porch and the street; Noah tagged along in silence, bless his heart, waiting for her to make the next move. Had to admit, an admirable quality in a man.

Did he have any idea how many tangled messages he'd

managed to deliver in those few sentences? Although, since he was, after all, a guy, she doubted it. Roxie had no idea whether to be flattered or annoyed. Disappointed or relieved. Although what he'd said about their not being right for each other was, and always would be, true—that whole attraction confession notwithstanding—what woman wants to hear she's being used to prove something to a guy's father? Even as a sidebar.

Even though the guy thinks she's hot.

Gonna chew on that one the rest of the night, aren'tcha?

Even so—and here was the weird part—she didn't doubt his sincerity for a second. Call it intuition, call it her reaction to that whole mess with Eden—whatever. But the man now walking beside her was not the same person who'd shown up to give the estimate a couple of weeks ago. Despite his balled up, backhanded explanation, Roxie really did believe he wanted to change.

And she could use a friend right now.

They'd reached the lousy sidewalk at the bottom of the stairs. Across the street, the light from Noah's folks' TV screen eerily pulsed through the drawn family room drapes, sending another wave of envy pulsing through her.

What was wrong with *her* tonight?

Hunching against the wind, she made a left turn down the road that eventually led to what passed as the center of town.

"Christmas lights'll be up soon," Noah observed as they walked, contentment evident in his voice. A hodgepodge of three centuries' worth of architectural styles plunked down along a series of twisting roads carved out of the mountain forest, Tierra Rosa was strictly a why-would-anyone-want-to-live-here? town…except for those who couldn't imagine living anywhere else.

"Have they changed any since we were in high school?"

"Not a lot, no." Then he chuckled. "Evangelista Ortega tried to put up icicle lights instead of luminarias a few years back. You wouldn't've believed the stink. She never tried it again."

"That's actually kind of scary," Roxie said, digging a knit hat out of her other pocket and ramming it over her curls, so aware of Noah's solid presence beside her she nearly trembled with it. "Being that resistant to change."

"A lot of folks might take issue with you on that. Keeping traditions going…it's comforting in a world that isn't much inclined to be comfortable. And not to push you or anything, but if you want to talk, you might want to think about getting started before we both turn into Popsicles."

"Who says I want to talk?" Except, when Noah shrugged, she said, "Trouble is, I don't know where *to* start."

"Just pick something and run with it. See where it takes you."

"To hell, in all likelihood," she muttered, then glanced at his shadowy profile. "Since I'm not real happy with myself right now." She sighed, the earlier scene in Charley's dining room replaying in her head. Ugh. "You sure you're up for this? Could get whiny."

"I'll take my chances. So why aren't you happy with yourself?"

She clamped shut her mouth. Noah nudged her with his elbow. "Go on."

"I…" She sucked in a breath. "Okay, I hate that I'm judging Eden on surface stuff. That I'm judging her at all. She can't help who she is, and for all I know there's a really good person under there."

"But that's not what your gut's telling you, is it?"

"Yeah, well, my gut's been wrong before. Except it's

just…Charley has no idea what easy pickings he is right now. And you must think I'm crazy."

"No, ma'am. I think you're a good niece who has every right to be concerned."

She snorted. "Not sure Charley sees it that way."

"Of course he doesn't. But that's not the point, is it?"

Roxie stole a glance at Noah's profile. She'd forgotten what it was like to have somebody in her corner. How good it felt.

How loath she was to trust it.

Stuffing her hands in her pockets, she muttered, "To tell the truth, I'm not sure what the point is anymore."

"Does Charley have anything worth picking, though? Besides the house? I'm sorry, I don't mean to pry—"

"No, I know you don't. You wouldn't," she said, giving him a little smile, catching one from him in return that wreaked serious havoc with her tum-tum. "And in any case, I'm talking about his heart, not his money. That…that he'll fall for her and then she'll see something sparklier over there and dump him. And he'll be devastated."

Not that she'd allow such a thing to happen to *her,* nope, havoc-wreaked tummies be damned.

Exhausted, Roxie sat on a low stone wall in front of somebody's house, ignoring the muffled yapping coming from behind a closed window. "As far as I know, Mae was Charley's only love. They met, they fell in love, they got married. No drama, no second-guessing, that was it. He has no idea what heartbreak is. Not that kind anyway."

Noah lowered himself onto the wall beside her. "And to play devil's advocate for a moment—"

"As if I haven't done that a thousand times in my own head for the past week."

"I know, but it might help to hear it outside your head. So let's see…from your standpoint, Charley's a clueless, vulnerable widower who's blinded by Eden's...vibrant personality."

"And her boobs."

"I wasn't gonna say that, but, okay, yeah. But what if we give him more credit than that? What if he knows exactly what he's doing? What if *he*'s playing *her*?"

Roxie's head snapped around. "Holy schmoly," she said, valiantly fighting not to be distracted by Noah's lovely, firm mouth mere inches away. "I hadn't even considered that."

"Right? I mean, sure, he's not exactly a spring chicken, and maybe he's inexperienced, but he's still a man. Maybe this is just a fling that'll burn itself out."

"Not that you'd know anything about that."

"Me? Nah."

Then, in the feeble glow from yapping mutt's porch light, she caught the grin, and it was cocky and endearing and she felt things she had no business feeling from a *friend* in general and Noah in particular.

Well, crap.

As if on cue, her cell phone rang. Jeff. Of course. Because this night hadn't been strange enough.

"You gonna get that?" Noah asked. Since, apparently, she was staring at the phone as if she'd never seen one of these newfangled things before.

"It's my ex."

"Then you should definitely get that. Otherwise you'll end up flinching every time the phone rings."

"Which you know all too well." He shrugged. "And if you answer and tell them to stop pestering you and they don't?"

"You get a new number."

Not wanting to know how many numbers Noah had probably gone through, over the past ten or so years, Roxie thought *I can do this,* and answered the phone.

Too late to catch the call, of course. Except this time, good ol' Jeffrey had left a voice mail.

Whoopee.

Noah discreetly stood again to give Roxie space while she listened to her ex's message, trying not to let on that his ass was frozen solid. And that he was having some serious, not-exactly-friendly thoughts about kissing her, which weren't doing a whole lot to bolster his self-esteem.

Her phone shoved back into her pocket, she jumped to her feet and started speed-walking down the sidewalk. Noah scurried to catch up, almost missing the "He wants my address," tossed over her shoulder.

"To…see you again?"

"Have no idea." She somehow sped up, which at least got the blood in Noah's butt moving again. "Not that there's a chance in hell of that."

"He cheat on you?"

"What? Oh. No. Well, not that I know of anyway." She kept going, her breath puffing in front of her face.

"Then—"

"Why did we break up? Because I got pregnant."

Noah stopped dead in his tracks. "You have a *kid?*" he said, only to realize of course she didn't. And that she wasn't happy about that. "Oh, hell. I'm sorry."

Turning, Roxie let out a brittle half laugh. "Oddly enough, Jeff wasn't. And Charley doesn't know. So please don't say anything."

"No, of course not—"

With a sharp nod and an even sharper turn, she continued down the street, practically at a trot by now, making Noah sprint behind her.

"Dammit, Rox—" Grabbing her shoulders, he spun her around. *"Stop."* At the tears glittering in her eyes, he loosened his grip. But when she averted her gaze, clearly retreating once more into her own little safe place, he said, "You know how the tiles were coming loose in Charley's bathroom? Easiest thing would've been to simply cement 'em back into place, call it a day. Except that wouldn't've solved the problem, since the loose tiles were only a symptom. The moldy wall behind it, *that* was the problem."

She frowned up at him. "Where are you going with this?"

Hopefully not straight to your S-list. "That...there's no point in trying to fix the surface stuff without cleaning up the mess underneath. All at once. Not in bits and pieces when the mood strikes. And yes, it's messy and potentially disgusting, and even scary because you don't know exactly what you're going to find, but better that than a crap job you're only gonna have to redo at some point down the road. I'm not afraid of what's under the surface, Rox. But if you don't open up all the way, let me see the mess, I can't fix it."

Her gaze danced with his for several seconds before she said, "What makes you think you can *fix* anything?"

"What makes you so sure I can't? Rox, honey," he said when she looked away again, "it's like you keep bringing me these loose tiles, like...you want me to know they're falling off, but you won't let me see why. Like you don't trust me or something—"

"It's not that!" she said, wide, startled eyes swinging back to his. "Ohmigosh, no! It's not *you*. It's just..." She swallowed. "I'm sorry for the fits and starts, I really am. But it's just been *me* for so long...."

When she pressed her lips together, Noah exhaled. Because, by rights, that was his cue to say, *It's okay, it doesn't have to be just you anymore, I'm here.* That he couldn't made him feel like a fraud.

"But it also feels good to be pushed out of my own head," she said.

"You sure?"

"No," she said on a short, soft laugh, then sighed. "Okay. When I said earlier that Charley has no idea how vulnerable he is? That's because…that was me, three years ago when I met Jeff." At Noah's frown, a sad smile curved her mouth. "See, I was engaged before. To this amazing, funny, sweet guy…who dropped dead of a freak aneurism at twenty-eight. A month before our wedding."

"Holy hell, Rox…"

Noah pulled her close, cupping her head against his chest, for the first time in his life feeling someone else's pain like it was his own. Not a pleasant sensation, God knows, but humbling. And oddly…gratifying. After a moment, though, she slipped out of his embrace and started walking again, only at a more normal pace this time. He took her hand; she didn't object.

"How is it you're even functioning?" he asked quietly. "After everything you've been through—"

"What? I should be curled up in a corner sucking my thumb?"

"Anybody else would be."

"Not my style. Although, yeah, Mac's death hit me pretty hard. Especially after losing my parents. But you know, I figured if I could come out the other side of that, I could do the same this time. That I *had* to. So about six months after Mac died, I forced myself to start dating again. That part was good. Better, anyway. Believing I'd fallen in love with the first man who reciprocated my interest—not so much."

"And that would be this…Jeff?"

She nodded. "He was very different from Mac. But I was so lonely, and still raw, and being with him seemed to fill the void. Not that I admitted that at the time," she said with a smirk. "The being raw part, I mean. If you'd asked me, I probably would've said I refused to see myself as a victim, that putting myself out there was my way of taking back my life. But the point is, I was so intent on filling that void I'd convinced myself Jeff just wasn't *sure* about having kids. Especially since, even though he was stunned about the pregnancy—heck, so was I, I was on the pill when it happened—he did seem to come around once the shock wore off. Or at least—and again—I heard what I wanted to hear."

Several seconds passed, their footsteps echoing in the silence, until she said, very softly, "Except I miscarried at twelve weeks. And Jeff's reaction? 'Probably for the best, right?'" She let out an equally soft, but obviously bitter, laugh. "Via a text message, no less."

"You're kidding?"

"Nope. And then—"

Now she turned all the way to Noah, anger and pain and disappointment colliding in her eyes. "Then he accused me of tricking him, of getting pregnant on purpose. Why he waited until then to unleash that particular fury, I have no idea—"

"Because he was a moron?"

"Yeah, well, I was in love with that moron. Thought I was, anyway. In any case, I trusted him. Except what I trusted was all in my imagination. What I wanted him to be. Which was who I'd lost," she said, her eyes brimming again. A hand shot up to stave off whatever Noah was about to say. "No, I'm fine," she said, her voice steadier. "The thing is, what I'd forgotten in my rush to get back to 'normal' is that there's no rushing the heart. It heals when it's ready, and not a moment before. Falling in love with someone—or thinking you have—when you're not yet over whoever came before, is a really, really bad idea. And Charley doesn't get that."

Maybe not. But Noah did. At least he understood now the sadness in Roxie's eyes, that she still mourned that first dude. And he hated the second one for *not* understanding that. For taking advantage of her.

"You have no idea," she said, the cold air snatching at her words, "how much I wanted that baby. Not that I was going to go out and get knocked up just because, I was never that far gone. But all this time the desire's been inside me, glowing like a little flame. You know?"

Ball's in your court, bud.

Uh, boy. He could be kind, or he could be honest. Although maybe, in this case, honesty was the kindest thing.

"No, actually. I don't." When Roxie tilted her head at him, he said, "Look, I would have never said to you what that butthead did. And if I'd gotten a gal pregnant, I would have dealt with it. But being a daddy has never been at the top of my list, either."

"Oh. But…" Her forehead creased. "I've seen you with your nieces and nephews—"

"Who mean the world to me, you bet. Just don't want kids of my own."

"I see," she said quietly. "Well. Thank you for being straight with me."

"One thing I've always been. So maybe you should stop blaming yourself for not hearing this Jeff when he said he didn't want kids. Because he obviously wasn't listening to you, either, when you said you did." He paused. "And by the way, if that Jeff character comes around here looking for you? He's liable to get knocked clear into next week."

Her laugh warmed him all the way through to his bones.

Chapter Six

Roxie let herself into the dark house, smacking at the switch by the front door that turned on the lamp beside the sofa, only to yelp when she saw her uncle stretched out in his recliner.

"Sorry," he mumbled, grabbing the lever to snap the chair upright. "Couldn't move fast enough to get a light on before you did."

"S'okay," she said, pressing her chest, partly because he'd scared the stuffing out of her, partly because that whole "friends" thing with Noah wasn't working. Except on an intellectual level, maybe. On a holy-smokes, it's-been-a-million-years-since-a-man-held-me level? Heh. Then she frowned. "Why are you sitting in the dark?"

"Thinking. What're you doing out this late?"

"Same thing. And it's not late, it's barely eight-thirty."

"You were out alone?"

"No, actually, Noah was with me." Since it wasn't exactly

a secret or anything. She unwound her scarf, hung it over the coatrack. Played it cool. "What happened to the movie?"

"I screwed up the schedule, it was half over by the time we got there. So we decided to call it a night. And what do you mean, Noah was with you?"

Her jacket joined the scarf as heat tracked up her neck, as if she was fifteen and had been caught necking with her boyfriend on the living room couch. Honestly. "We needed to walk off the pizza. Got a problem with that?"

"Something going on between you?"

Roxie tugged down her sweater sleeve. "No," she said. Because it was true, for one thing. And for another, she wasn't a big fan of repeating her mistakes. Which their conversation had reinforced all too clearly, thank you.

"Too bad. He's a nice boy."

It took a second. Then Roxie barked out a laugh. "Less than two weeks ago you warned me away from him."

Her uncle grinned. Mischievously. "Less than two weeks ago I hadn't met Eden."

Oh, Lord. "Yes, Noah's a nice guy," she said, turning on another light, "but setting aside the fact that he's not even remotely interested in marriage, kids, all that fun stuff, we have absolutely nothing in common. You want anything?"

"Yeah. For you to like Eden."

Well. At least Noah had been booted out of the conversation. Apparently.

"Oh, Charley…" Roxie sat in the chair facing him, setting her phone on the coffee table. Trying not to squint from all the glowing across from her. "I want to. No, I really do. I just…" Crap. "Do you honestly know what you're getting into?" she said gently. "Eden's kind of…not Mae."

Chuckling softly, Charley leaned back in the sofa, cradling his probably cold tea and looking pretty much on top of the world. His face even looked fuller. "Noticed that right off, didja?"

"Kinda hard to miss."

His smile faded as his gaze sharpened. "Not looking for a clone of my dead wife, you know."

"I wasn't aware you were looking for anything."

"I wasn't. It just happened."

Let it go, girl, let it—"Are you two really serious?"

"Serious enough she wants to cook Thanksgiving dinner for us. At her place."

"Oh. Wow. And you're sure…I'm invited?"

"For God's sake, Rox—why are you being like this?"

"Because I love you and I don't want to see you hurt?"

"Not because it hurts *you* to see me happy?"

It took a second or two to get to her feet and start out of the room, although this was stupid, she had no right to take umbrage when she'd thought virtually the same thing less than an hour before….

"Rox," Charley said on a sigh. "Come back here."

Nearly to the door, she turned, hugging herself. Knowing what he was going to say. So she preempted him. "Despite what you think, this isn't about me—"

"That's right, it isn't," her uncle said, standing as well, his posture more erect, his shoulders more square than they'd been in the past several months. "You want to be cautious about your own relationships after what happened? You go right ahead. You've earned that right. But that right doesn't extend to anyone else. Especially me. And I refuse to make my decisions based on *your* fears."

For a moment she simply stood there, assaulted by a maelstrom of emotions—embarrassment, mostly, at having her face so thoroughly rubbed in the truth. But she also found herself admiring her uncle's damn-the-torpedoes courage, not only for taking on Eden, but for putting his heart out there again, period.

Didn't exactly make her feel proud of herself for dragging her feet about facing Jeff. An oversight she silently vowed to remedy ASAP.

But for now…hot *damn* she was proud of Charley. And he needed to know that.

She crossed the room, seeing surprise flash in his eyes a moment before she wrapped her arms around his waist, laying her head against his chest. "I apologize," she said, then looked up at him. "And I'm going to be pleased for you if it kills me. I am," she said at his chuckle. "Still. It's so…sudden."

Draping one skinny arm around her shoulders, Charley steered her to the sofa, where, once seated, she leaned into his side like she used to with her father when she was little. Like she'd wanted to with Charley right after her parents died, except stubbornness and pain and fear wouldn't let her.

"I have no idea where this is going, Rox," he said into her hair. "But at Edie's and my age, we don't have the luxury of taking things slowly. All I know is, we have *fun* together, and she makes me feel twenty years younger. Yes, she's crazy, but after everything I went through with your aunt… maybe a little crazy isn't such a bad thing."

She almost laughed, then sighed. "I still worry about you."

"Well, don't. I'm fine. And if I get my heart broken—" she felt him shrug "—you can tell me 'I told you so.' How's that?"

"Deal," she said, then sat up to pick her buzzing phone off the coffee table.

"So you coming to Thanksgiving or not?"

"Of course I'll come to Thanksgiving," she said, frowning

at the text from the unrecognized number. Beside her, her
uncle hmmphed. The man was hardly a Luddite; he'd been
working with computers long before they made them small
enough to fit in the palm of your hand. But he never missed
an opportunity to give her grief about being attached to her
phone 24/7.

"Ohmigosh," she said, blinking to make sure she'd read
the message correctly.

"For heaven's sake, girl! What—"

"It's from the owner of this fabulous gallery in Atlanta!
They got my resume and want me to come out for an interview! Ohmigod, Charley!" With a squeal, she lunged
sideways to give him another hug. "I finally got a nibble!
If this works out, I'll finally be out of your hair! Won't that
be great?"

"Uh, yeah," he said. Except he didn't look nearly as
thrilled about the prospect of her leaving the house, of leaving Tierra Rosa, as she might have thought.

And the kicker was, Roxie wasn't nearly as thrilled about
that as she might have thought, either.

Well, hell.

Noah told himself he'd crossed the street to his parents'
house for one reason, and one reason only: food. There was
always something to eat there. As opposed to his place,
which put Old Mother Hubbard's cupboard to shame. So sue
him, he hated grocery shopping. Too damn many choices,
he always came out with a bunch of junk he didn't need
and usually ended up not liking, anyway.

He'd come to a standstill in his parents' small foyer,
thinking that over while Blue whined and wriggled at his
knees for some loving. Because some people, he mused as
he idly patted the rhapsodic mutt, had no trouble knowing
what they liked, what they needed, when they went into

the store. If they went in for vegetables, they didn't get distracted by the donuts. Or at least they didn't get so distracted by the donuts they forgot the broccoli. Didn't feel as if they were missing something when they left, either.

Must be nice, being that focused. Knowing who you were, what you wanted....

"Hey, honey," his mother whispered, creeping toward him in her winter uniform of a loose sweatshirt, leggings and sheepskin booties, her fading red hair loose around her still-smooth face. "Blue, for heaven's sake, a person'd think you were the most neglected dog in the world. What're you doing here?" she said, accepting Noah's hug.

"Scavenging. Where's Dad?"

"Asleep," she said, following Noah and Blue into the country-style kitchen that needed updating nearly as much as Charley's. Except in Noah's opinion the blue-and-dark-red color scheme wore somewhat better than seventies bilious.

"It's barely nine."

"I know." She pulled a casserole of some kind out of the fridge. "But that project is whipping his butt. Poor guy ate dinner, watched a half hour of the sports channel and conked out in his chair. He looked so peaceful I tossed an afghan over him and left him there." Noah came up beside her to lift the foil on what looked like lasagna, while an expectantly quivering Blue planted his butt far enough away to not get stepped on, but still close enough so nobody'd forget him, either. When Donna went for a knife, though, Noah took it out of her hand.

"I came for food, not for you to wait on me."

"I wait on you today," she said, reclaiming the knife, "you change my diapers tomorrow. Fair trade. Now go sit." She cut him a big chunk of the lasagna, clunked the covered plate in the microwave. "You want some salad? It's already made."

"Sure." Noah slid into the sturdy wooden chair at the table that'd been there his entire life, the familiarity of the kitchen, his parents, even the dog, settling like a warm blanket over him. Strange, how for somebody whose longest relationship so far had lasted maybe three months, he wasn't real big on change in any other aspect of his life.

Lord, a therapist would have a field day with him, he mused as he scratched the dog's ears, the head belonging to the ears now wedged between Noah's thigh and the table.

His mother slid the plate in front of him, heaped with fragrant, gooey lasagna on one side and her everything-she-had-on-hand salad on the other. "Blue! Go! You know better than that!" The dog slunk off to collapse with a put-upon moan by the stove, biding his time until the Big Bad Woman wasn't watching to sneak right back for a handout. "So how's Charley's house reno coming along?" Donna asked, sitting opposite him with a cup of something Noah doubted he'd like.

"Pretty good, all told. Kitchen demo'll be done tomorrow, we start tiling right after. Cabinets and countertops won't be in for a few days, though."

"Your father says you're supervising the whole job? Even the cabinetry?"

"Yep."

"Lord, it's about time," Donna said on an exhale. "I've been on his case for I don't know how long about him needing to give you more responsibility."

This was news. "You have?"

She nodded. "But you know your father. Pigheaded as they come. Oh, while I'm thinking about it—why don't you invite Charley and Roxie here for family dinner on Thursday night? They don't have a *kitchen*," she said before Noah could protest. "It's the Christian thing to do. And speaking of Roxie…" Her cheek nestled in her hand, she smiled. "I hear she's been a big help."

Noah shoveled a bite of lasagna into his mouth, refusing to take his mother's bait. Never mind that he couldn't get Roxie's scent, or the feel of her in his arms, or her teary eyes when she told him about her past, out of his head. But for damn sure he wasn't about to share any of that with his mother.

So, "Yeah, she sure has," was all he offered as he got up to pour himself a glass of milk. When he returned to the table, the smile hadn't faded one bit. *Tough,* he thought, forking in a bunch of leaves and…stuff, then kicking back several swallows of milk. "Charley say anything to you guys about that gal he's dating?"

His mother's hand crashed to the table loud enough to rouse the dog. "Charley's *dating?* Who?"

"Nobody you know. Some gal from Santa Fe."

"You met her?"

"Sorta. I was still at the house tonight when they came in."

"She nice?"

"She's…different. Used to be on Broadway. Long time ago."

"Broadway? You don't say." Donna sat back in her chair with her arms crossed, as if she was trying to process all this. "Well. Good for him, I suppose. What does Roxie think?"

"Roxie's…" Twiddling his fork in his fingers, Noah weighed his words. "She's got some stuff in her past that might be coloring the way she looks at the situation."

"She doesn't like her."

"She doesn't *trust* her." At his mother's arched brow, he

said, "And I've already said more than I should. So if you don't mind, can we just leave it?"

"You brought up the subject."

Yeah, desperation will do that. "I know. But...I probably should'nt've."

"Interesting," Donna said, an inscrutable smile pushing at her high cheekbones. "Roxie sharing things you can't talk about with your own mother."

"Mom. No."

Donna laughed and covered his free hand with her own. "You are so much fun to torment, you know that—?"

"Thought I heard voices," his father said, yawning as he chuffed into the kitchen. Shaking his head, he opened his eyes too wide. "Guess I passed out. There any more of that?" he said, nodding toward Noah's nearly empty plate.

"Right on the counter, help yourself," Donna said. "Although not too much, or you'll be up all night with indigestion." Behind his wife's back, Gene rolled his eyes for Noah's benefit. "And you can quit it with the eye rolling right now, Eugene Garrett!" Then, while Noah chuckled around his last bite, she twisted around to face his dad. "Did you know Charley was dating somebody?"

Getting up to help himself to a piece of apple pie on the counter, Noah listened to his parents' conversation, as soothing and predictable as always. The sound of best friends, of true partners. Again, like with the grocery shopping thing, he felt a prickle that was almost envy, not exactly for what they had as much as for who they were.

What the hell was going on with him tonight?

A little later he said his goodbyes and walked out into the night, reminding himself that right now his brothers were all probably struggling to get kids asleep in houses strewn with toys, that they couldn't simply leave when the mood struck. That in a few minutes Noah would walk into his apartment, and it would be empty and quiet, and he could walk across the floor without impaling his foot on a Lego piece or something, and he could sleep naked—hell, he could *walk around* naked if he wanted—without worrying about impressionable little minds.

Then he thought about Roxie, the pain in her eyes when she talked about her first fiancé, the baby she'd lost, about his reaction of wanting to make it better, make her better, and how that didn't jibe at all with everything, anything, he'd ever thought about himself.

And here he'd always assumed that things got clearer as you got older.

So much for that.

By the time Noah got to Charley's the next morning, Roxie had already stripped a good chunk of the stairwell wallpaper, a project that must've taken hours already.

"You even go to bed last night?" he called up the stairs, his renegade heart going *ka-thump* when she grinned down at him.

"I was up at four. Couldn't sleep."

"Meaning I was up at four, too," Charley muttered from the head of the stairs. Dressed in neatly pressed khakis, a blue button-down shirt open at the collar and a heavy brown cardigan that didn't droop from his shoulders nearly as much as it would've even a couple of weeks ago, the older man jerked his head in Roxie's direction as he passed her on the way down. "Girl's got news."

"Oh?" Noah said, his stomach crashing as he hurtled to the conclusion that The Moron and she had patched things up. What the hell?

"I might have a job! In Atlanta!"

More stomach crashing. But again…what the hell? Wasn't

like he hadn't known all along she'd be blowing this joint sooner or later. Besides which, *there was nothing going on between them*.

Then she bounced downstairs, eyes sparkling, face glowing, curls bobbing, and he just thought, *Hell*. "It's for this really chi-chi gallery. They want me to come for an interview next week! So, by the way, I won't be here Friday." Man, that grin was bright. "Isn't it *wonderful*?"

Then she threw her arms around his neck and hugged him.

"Don't take it personally," Charley said. "She's hugging everything in sight."

"That's…really great," Noah finally said, trying not to react to all that enthusiastic, sweet-smelling softness pressing against him, then setting her apart before she realized exactly how well that was not working. "You must be real excited."

Behind them, Charley grunted as Roxie bubbled, "You have no idea! And *Atlanta!*" Then she took him by the shoulders and planted a kiss on his cheek. Lord, he half expected her to twirl around and burst into song. Instead, she clasped her hands and said, "I think this calls for Evangelista's cinnamon rolls and breakfast burritos, don't you?"

"I'll go," Charley said, trekking to the front door, obviously seizing the opportunity to escape.

"Bring back enough for everybody! Silas and Jesse, too, they said they'd be here this morning!" Roxie shouted after him, then released a happy sigh. Until she must have seen something in Noah's face that made her happy to take a hike. "What's wrong?"

"Nothing. Except I *haven't* been up since four, so I'm not firing on all jets yet. So. Wow. Atlanta. That's…far."

"I know," she said dreamily, drifting back up the stairs with a goony smile on her face. "Oh, by the way…" She leaned over to look at the front door, even though they'd both heard her uncle's truck roar off. "Charley and I had a heart-to-heart last night. About Eden. And I realized…I have to let it go. That it's not up to me to protect him."

"And that maybe he doesn't need anybody protecting him?"

"That, too," she said over the sound of another swath of old wallpaper biting the dust.

"But you're still worried."

"Like you wouldn't believe. Still." She cut the air with one hand. "I'm done."

Noah leaned on the banister. "You call back your ex?"

Her eyes bounced to his, then back to the wall. "And ruin this good mood? No way."

"Rox—"

"I know, I know. And I will. I swear. But not right now."

Noah thought for a moment. Decided to spit it out anyway. "Would it help if I was around when you did?"

Big old eyes flashed to his. "No! I mean, that's very sweet, but…" Shaking her head, she slapped a wet sponge against the next piece of wallpaper. "I have to do this by myself."

"Who says?"

She frowned down at him. "Who says what?"

"That you have to deal with him on your own." *And you're setting yourself up for getting closer to the woman, why?*

"I do," she said, tossing the sponge into a bucket on the landing, then wiping her hands on a towel before sitting on the stairs a few feet above him. "Because I was the one who ran. Well, after I kicked him out of our apartment. And to be fair, I think he deserves an explanation. If not an apology."

Noah's brow knotted. "Sounds to me like he doesn't *deserve* anything. Except a swift kick in the ass, maybe."

"Already did that. Not literally, of course. But he got the message. So I'm thinking this is for me."

See, this is why female logic eluded him. "How can you apologizing to him be *for* you?"

She leaned back on her elbows, a crease digging into the space between her brows. "Because our relationship was a mistake. A mistake that would've never happened if I'd been honest with myself. And with him. If I hadn't gotten involved for the wrong reasons."

"But what he said to you—"

"Was cold and unfeeling and reprehensible. Absolutely. But even if he'd been kinder about it, things eventually would have fallen apart, anyway. And the reasons behind that were every bit as much my fault as his. That's all I'm saying."

On a sigh, Noah came to sit on the step right below hers, leaning forward so as to leave enough space between them for it not to be awkward. For her, at least. "That job offer really put you in a good mood, huh?"

Her laugh was soft. "It definitely did. But I'd already come to that conclusion about Jeff and me."

"You're something else, you know that?"

He felt her gaze on the side of his face, followed by a shrug. "Only trying to muddle through life like everybody else."

Maybe so. But clearly her muddling skills were better than most. Especially Noah's.

"So when you gonna call him?" he asked, quickly standing when his loud, chatterbox brothers walked through the door. Roxie stood as well, lightly tripping down the stairs to give them both hugs. Charley hadn't been kidding.

"Soon," Rox promised, tossing Noah a smile over her

shoulder, earning him quizzical looks from both his siblings. "When it feels right."

And for a moment, assuming Jeff the Jerk wanted to make amends, Noah almost felt sorry for him, that he was stupid enough to screw up what he'd had.

Almost.

If nothing else, seeing Eden every day gave Charley the perfect excuse to get out of the house, leaving Noah and Rox and the crew to the chaos. Not that he needed an excuse to visit his *girlfriend,* he thought, with what was probably a dumb grin, as he drove toward Santa Fe.

He wasn't sure, at least not yet, that what he felt for Eden was love, exactly. Not like he'd felt for Mae, that was for sure. Maybe he *was* infatuated. And maybe that's all it ever would be. But what he'd said to Rox about Eden making him happy? That was true enough. Because she made him forget the pain. Not Mae. He'd never forget her. Just the pain. And why that was a bad thing?

He pulled into Eden's apartment complex's parking lot, getting a little thrill when she waved from her balcony, her face all lit up. Although her yelling, "Yoo-hoo!" at the top of her lungs he could live without, truth be told. He could definitely understand Rox's reservations—the woman wasn't exactly a shrinking violet.

She vanished inside to greet him at her front door, giving him a big kiss on the lips, which was as far as their sex life went at this point. Not that she wasn't amenable to something more down the road, she'd said, but what with their being still newish to widowhood and all, she thought it best they wait. For what, Charley wasn't sure.

"So what do you think?" she said, spinning around in the cramped living room to show off what he assumed was one of her new creations, something that couldn't decide if it was a blouse or dress or what, worn over a pair of those skinny pants that made her feet look big. Not that he would tell her that. As usual, she'd overdone her strong, spicy perfume. Mostly it didn't bother him, but he did occasionally consider suggesting she take it down a notch—or two—only to immediately rethink that. Women rarely took kindly to what could easily be construed as criticism of their personal hygiene.

"Very nice," Charley said, smiling when Eden grinned back, even though that little Chihuahua of hers growled at Charley's feet. He'd never been a big fan of tiny dogs, but Eden was devoted to the thing, so he supposed he could get used to her.

"For goodness' sake, Diva," Eden said, scooping the little rat dog into her arms. "You act like you've never seen the man! Go on, give him some love." Thankfully, for both dog and him, she didn't actually thrust the poor creature into Charley's face—a move which would have probably resulted in Charley's losing his nose—but when she offered up her "baby" the beast did seem amenable to a quick scratch behind the ears.

"I made chicken salad inside a cranberry Jell-O mold," she said, setting the dog down and moving to her eating nook, the bistro table all set for two. "Hope that's okay, I got the recipe out of a magazine."

Still full from two burritos and a cinnamon roll earlier, Charley smiled. "Sounds perfect."

He sat while, humming to herself, Eden bustled and fussed in the kitchen, a woman apparently content in her world. Content with him, he thought on a small burst of pleasure. Her garment billowing like a benign jellyfish around her, she swept back into the living area and set the half-size serving platter in the center of the table with a "Ta-da!"

"Wow. That looks amazing," Charley said, and she flushed, pleased.

While Eden settled across from him, Charley waited to see if Mae had something to say about all of this. But no. In fact, his wife hadn't talked to him since the one time, when she'd told him to fix Rox. Not that he or anybody else could "fix" the girl anymore than he'd let his niece dictate the terms of his relationship with Eden. And if she got this job, he'd be genuinely happy for her. Except there was something decidedly off about her excitement. Like it was a little too forced, maybe. And he was betting that "something" had to do with Noah—

"Everything okay?" Delicately salting her chicken salad, bracelets jangling, Eden cast a smile in his direction while the dog peered bug-eyed at Charley from her lap.

"Thinking about Roxie," he said, eagerly digging in despite his lack of appetite. Woman definitely knew her way around the kitchen, that was for sure. Although her dishes tended more toward the exotic than Mae's—there was some spice or other in here he didn't recognize—but it was pretty good.

"Is she coming for Thanksgiving?"

"She said she would."

"Willingly?"

Nodding, Charley forked in a second bite, then took a taste of the cranberry mold. Not bad. But he did not feel up to going into his and Rox's conversation the night before. "She's got a job interview next week. In Atlanta."

"Really?" Eden plucked a small, knotted roll from the basket beside the platter, slathered on a good helping of low-fat spread. "She must be over the moon."

"She is."

"But you're not."

About to grab one of the rolls, Charley stopped, his gaze darting to hers. "What makes you say that?"

The slippery fabric slipped off one freckled shoulder when she shrugged. "You're not exactly a closed book, Charley." She pinched off a chunk of roll and popped it into her mouth. "And I bet I know somebody else who wouldn't be happy if she left," she said, waving the uneaten part of the roll at him, the dog's head bobbing along. "That Noah."

"Noah?" Not that Charley didn't suspect the same thing, his niece's protests that there was nothing between them notwithstanding. A blind man could see they were attracted to each other. Because he *was* a nice boy, despite his reputation. Good-looking, too, Charley supposed. But after his and Rox's talk last night he'd got to thinking, that after what she'd been through with that Jeff, it'd take more than *nice* and *good-looking* to sweep the gal off her feet again. "Rox'd never have him," he said mildly. "Not her type."

"Doesn't mean she's not his."

Suddenly the very thing about Eden that had hooked him to begin with—her boldness—wasn't sitting all that well. But he couldn't exactly tell her she was butting into private family business, could he? So instead, he said, "Only because she's female, most likely. Rumor has it boy's got more oats to sow than ten men combined. He could never make Roxie—or, I'm guessing, any other gal—happy. At least not in the long run."

"Except you'd said yourself, when we were driving last night, that he seems to have changed in a lot of ways."

"Did I?"

"Yes, you did. So maybe he's growing up. It does happen, you know. My Sal, you should've seen him in his early twenties. Wild? You have no idea. Then suddenly he hits twenty-seven, twenty-eight, and boom! Like night and day.

Thirty-five years we were married, and never once did he so much as flirt with another woman. And I know what you're thinking—how can I be sure?"

She took a sip of her iced tea. "Because these things, they never stay a secret. The guy trips up, or somebody always blabs, whatever. Especially after the funeral. That seems to be when the hitherto unknown mistresses come crawling outta the woodwork." Her head wagged. "Not with Sal. So sometimes people do change. And you know…" Her gaze averted, she picked at her gelatin. "Having her settled…well, it would take a huge load off your mind, wouldn't it?"

Charley looked up, the Jell-O quivering on his fork. "What's that supposed to mean?"

"Oh, come on, Charley! She's what, thirty? And not even your daughter! It's not right, you worrying over her like she's still a child! Or her acting like you're still one! You both deserve your own lives, don't you think?"

Funny, how thoughts that make perfect sense inside your own head sound not so perfect coming out of somebody else's mouth. Because for all Edie had virtually echoed Charley's own take on the subject, the flare of annoyance setting ablaze the chicken and gelatin in his stomach made him realize things weren't nearly that black and white.

"For one thing," he said, "it's not up to me to get her 'settled.'" *Or fix her,* he silently added to his wife, in case she was listening in. "Whether Noah really is changed or not, I have no idea. But that's for Rox to decide, not me. Or anybody else. For another, maybe she's not blood kin, but she's the closest thing to a daughter Mae and I ever had. Nor do I recall there being an age cutoff for when you stop being concerned about somebody."

Her cheeks pinker than usual, Edie leveled him with her gaze. "I'm sorry if I overstepped. I'm just afraid…" Petting the dog, she sagged back in her chair. "She doesn't like me,

Charley. And my gut tells me she'll do anything she can to break us up."

"She doesn't *know* you, Edie," he said, thinking, with a start, *And obviously she's not the only one.* "Yes, we worry about each other. And it's sometimes annoying as hell. But we don't get in each other's business. I can promise you no matter what she thinks she would never interfere—"

"Maybe not overtly," Eden said, her eyes shiny. "But believe me—" she pressed one hand to her chest "—and I'm only speaking as another woman, here—if she thinks I'm bad for you she'll wear you down until you think it, too. Especially as long as she's still single herself!" At Charley's probably flummoxed expression, Edie lifted her chin. "Sorry, but I can't keep this inside. And I feel like I'm on really shaky ground here, with her."

A long moment passed before Charley folded his napkin, placing it carefully beside his plate before getting to his feet, thinking it wasn't Roxie she was on shaky ground with right now. "I like you, Edie. A lot. But if you're convinced I can't think for myself, or tell the difference between manipulation and being cared about…that's a deal breaker. Believe *me*," he said, his eyes on hers, "I can. Thanks for lunch," he mumbled, then started for the door.

"Charley?"

When he turned she was practically on top of him, clutching her little dog and looking quite distressed. Moved—and frankly torn—Charley laid a hand on her cheek. "I don't see my niece as either a burden or an obstacle. As long as you do, however…" He took a deep breath. "If you don't trust *me,* maybe it's best if we take a break."

Then he kissed her on her soft, fragrant cheek and left, realizing with a kick to his gut that following your conscience doesn't necessarily mean you're going to be happy about it.

Chapter Seven

In front of Roxie stood a grinning, wriggling little boy wearing well-worn blue jeans, a heavyweight hoodie and straw-colored, choir boy bangs. Beside him stood an unshaven Noah wearing well-worn jeans—black, natch—a heavyweight hoodie…and a smaller boy in plush, dinosaur-splotched footed jammies, clinging to him like a limpet.

It was a lot to take in at seven-thirty in the morning. Especially given her lack of sleep over the pending job interview, her screwing up the courage to call Jeff *and* her uncle's two-days-and-counting mopefest, which she assumed had something to with Eden but God forbid he actually talk to her or anything.

"Sorry," Noah mumbled as he ushered in his six-year-old nephew, Ollie, then gently set a still very sleepy, two years younger Tad on the sofa, along with a jumble of pint-size clothes and a largish paper bag smelling of greasy heaven. "Silas had an early appointment and Jewel's out at a birth.

So I said I'd get Ollie to school by nine, and whichever one finishes up first'll swing by to collect Tad. Hope that's not a problem? Ollie!" he shouted as the boy vanished into the back of the house. "Get back here!"

"Coming!"

"Of course not," Roxie said, aching to take the sagging little boy in her arms, even as she kept an eye on his brother, darting from room to room like a pinball, his backpack going *thunkathunkathunka* between his slender shoulders, his sneakers pounding against the bare wooden floors.

First things first, though. "Hey, I called—"

"What's all that racket?" Charley called from upstairs. Blast.

"Silas's boys are here for a little while," Roxie called back up. "Come say hi!"

Slam.

Crouching in front of the wobbly kid, who was seriously listing east, Noah shot her a glance. "Still?"

"Yeah," she said on a sigh. "Um, I—"

"Tad! Wake up, buddy!"

Shaking his curly head, the little boy collapsed into a ball on the sofa cushion, hands smushed underneath his cheek. Roxie gave up. For the time being, anyway. "You want me to set out plates and stuff for the boys?"

"Nah, paper bags, fingers—we're good. Okay, Tadpole," Noah said, heaving the kid upright again, "I need to get you dressed—"

"Don'wanna," the pink-cheeked tyke said on a huge yawn, drooping forward to crumple against his uncle's chest, thumb in mouth, eyes drifting shut again.

"I know, guy," Noah said, real softly, rubbing the little back, and Roxie could actually feel her heart melting. And her knees. And…other things. "But you gotta. Aren't you hungry?"

With a slow, curl-quivering head shake, the squirt cuddled closer. Chuckling, Noah gently untangled the little arms, letting Tad slump against the back of the sofa to tug off his pj bottoms…earning himself a shriek of laughter when he tickled the soles of the little guy's feet. Meanwhile, Ollie thunked and clumped back and forth, back and forth, back and forth…

"You're good at that," Roxie said to Noah, snatching up the bag of food before the grease reached the sofa, carrying it to the one end of the dining table not covered in Mae's stuff and renovation detritus.

"What? Dressing kids?" Noah yanked a long-sleeve T-shirt over Tad's head. Not looking at her. "Line up limbs to corresponding openings in clothes, how hard could it be?" The little boy blinked, then grinned, and Roxie could practically see the jets firing, one by one. Countdown to liftoff in three…two…one…

"Shoes!" Noah boomed, grabbing Tad before he could take off after his brother. Feet rammed into a pair of SpongeBob sneakers, the little one let out a war whoop and threw his entire small self at the bigger one, igniting an instant wrestling match. In one sweet move Noah surged to his feet and yanked the two apart; Roxie tried to swallow her laughter, but a muffled snort still escaped.

"Knock it off, you two!" Noah pointed at the table. "Go, sit!"

This said with a mock stern look at the giggling boys, who flew into the dining room, chairs shimmying dangerously as they scrambled up into them, and then Noah was calmly divvying up egg sandwiches and hash browns and pint-size milk cartons between the two wiggle worms, and Roxie thought, *Yes, please, just like that,* although of course she didn't mean exactly like that, since Noah would never—

Because he wasn't—

Girl, don't even go there.

"There's plenty," Noah said to her, unwrapping his own sandwich as he sat at right angles to his nephews. "Help yourself."

Honest to Pete. Roxie plucked a bunch of napkins off the sideboard and distributed them, then pulled a still-warm sandwich out of the bag. "Mae used to make these," she said with a blissful sigh, as she settled across from the boys. "I tried once, but it was a spectacular failure."

Chewing, Noah frowned at her. "You can't make an egg sandwich?"

"I can barely make toast. I can, however, identify a piece of antique glassware down to the decade, so I'm not entirely useless. So, where'd you get these?"

"Jewel made 'em, I'm guessing. Silas sort of shoved them at me when I walked through the door. Tad, sit up, buddy, you're gonna fall out of the chair—"

"Ahmjushtryingtosee—"

"Don't talk with your mouth full."

The preschooler's arm jutted toward the window as he gulped down his bite. "That is like the *biggest* crow *ever!*"

Noah caught Oliver with one hand before the kid fell out of his chair trying to get a better look; then all three traipsed to the window, where Noah let out a long, low whistle. "Holy moly, you ain't whistling Dixie! Rox, get over here and look at this sucker!"

When she did, Noah put his hand on her waist to steer her to the right spot, and she thought, *Okay, maybe that's not such a good idea,* even before the skin-searing, hoo-hah tingling *zing!* that all too smartly reminded her exactly why celibacy sucked. Especially when it wasn't by choice. Except, as he moved away, the vivid memory of her surreal

phone conversation last night reminded her that, in her experience, the alternative—as in, intimacy with the wrong
person for the wrong reasons—sucked far more.

Yes, it did.

The space shuttle-size bird duly admired by all, Noah
got the boys settled back in their chairs, then snapped his
fingers. "I keep forgetting…Mom wants you and Charley
to come over for family dinner Thursday night," he said,
and Roxie's instant reaction was *Oh, heck, no,* until he
added, "because you're currently kitchenless," and she remembered there'd be a million Garretts there—Noah and
she probably wouldn't even see each other. And she was
getting really sick of microwave dinners with mushy rice
and limp broccoli—

Roxie heard Charley's floor creak overhead, then his
door *eerrrk* open. And close again. Softly. As though he
didn't want anyone to know he *so* wanted one of those egg
sandwiches.

Sighing, she glanced at the kids, who were busy having
a who-can-stuff-the-most-food-in-his-mouth contest, then
said, "If I can pry Charley out of his bedroom by then,
sure—"

"We're done," Ollie said, scrubbing his greasy napkin
across his mouth. "C'n we go outside?"

"Yeah, c'n we?"

"I don't know, guys," Noah said, but Roxie laughed.

"The backyard's fenced. Not much harm they can do,"
she said.

To which Noah replied, "Remember you said that," and
they were off at top speed through the kitchen and out the
door.

They both took a moment to absorb the silence before
she said, "All he does is sit in his room, listening to old
opera recordings," while watching Noah efficiently gather

the leftover debris and stuff it back into the paper bag. "I see evidence of his sneaking down to raid the fridge in the middle of the night, or going out for food while I'm at work, but other than that, he's turned into a mole."

"You think it's over?"

"Who knows? But now he's back in grump mode. I swear, it almost makes me wish Eden was still in the picture, because he's reminding me a lot of me when I was a teenager and some boy or other blew me off."

Noah gave her a look. "Like me?"

"Actually, I was thinking of Sammy Rodriquez," she lied, thinking she already had more than enough pots on the stove without stirring that one, thank you. "Speaking of former boyf—"

"Knock, knock!" came a perky female voice from the entryway, before, a moment later, Silas's windblown fiancée appeared at the dining room doorway, her little glasses fogged from coming from the cold into the heated house. "False alarm, no baby yet." A symphony of color in bright blue leggings, red high-top sneakers and a multicolored paisley jacket, Jewel glanced around.

"You lose 'em somewhere? Ah," she said as shrieks from the backyard found their way into the house. "Thanks, guy," she said to Noah, dimpling at him as she reached up to give him a quick peck on the cheek. "You're the best."

Yes, you are, dammit, Roxie thought despondently, as Jewel gathered her stepsons-to-be and herded them out to her car, around the same time the crew's assorted trucks and vans began pulling up outside, and the slamming of doors, the shouted greetings officially heralded the start of a new workday. With a grin, Noah started out of the room. "Showtime—"

"I called Jeff."

His head whipped around. "Why didn't you say something sooner?"

"I've been trying to!"

"So...what...?"

She took a deep breath. "We talked for maybe three minutes. He said, again, he wanted to see me. I said no, no point, delivered my little speech and...that was that. Except for his saying he'd found a couple of old CDs of mine mixed up with his, could he have my address so he could mail them back to me?"

Odd. If she hadn't known better, Roxie would have sworn she saw a little *"Thank you, Lord,"* flash in Noah's eyes. "Did he at least sound brokenhearted that you'd refused him?"

"Not really, no. But then, dude's got an ego like a bomb shelter."

The front door, already left ajar, burst open, followed by heavy, work-booted footfalls, more laughter, the hum of energy enveloping a half dozen men focused on what they had to do. Noah glanced toward the noise, then back at Roxie, his voice barely more than a whisper when he spoke. "You okay?"

Such a simple question, but so heartfelt it nearly brought tears to her eyes. "I think so. I'd expected...actually, I don't know what I expected, exactly. But something. Regret? Anger?" She shook her head. "It was weird. I felt absolutely...nothing. As though none of it had ever happened, really. Except for...well. You know. The baby."

Noah's gaze darkened, for barely a moment, before a slight smile curved his mouth. "Now aren't you glad you called?"

"Yeah," she said on whooshed breath. "I am."

The smile softened. "I'm real proud of you, Rox—"

"Hey, Noah—" One of his crew stuck his dark-haired

head in the kitchen. "We brought the new cabinets. You installing them today?"

Ever since they'd started this project, Roxie had been all too aware of the obvious respect Noah's crew had for their boss. And he for them. Not once had she heard them talking trash about him behind his back, or seen them goof off when he wasn't there, nor had he ever complained about any of them in her presence. In fact, the more she got to know him, the more she saw the rock-solid core beneath the cocky exterior…and the more he reminded her of what she'd loved about Mac. Not personality-wise—in that respect, they couldn't have been more different—but integrity? Honesty? Fairness? They might as well have been twins.

Except, lest she carry this twin thing too far, Mac had wanted to be a father. And even she wasn't naive enough to confuse Noah's devotion to his brothers' kids for a suppressed desire to have his own. So, falling for the guy would be pointless and dumb and frustrating, especially since she'd been down that particular dead-end road once before.

Noah tore his gaze away—dear God, how long had they been staring at each other?—to nod at the baby-faced young man in a flannel shirt grinning at him. "Sure are, let's get 'em in." Then he turned to Roxie. "Ready to lend a hand?"

She blanched. Stripping wallpaper and mutilating tile was one thing. Actually helping to install something that could fall on someone's head if she screwed up?

"I'm not sure—"

"You'll be fine, Miss Roxie," the kid said. "Mr. Noah would never let you make a mistake."

Then she met Mr. Noah's mischief-filled eyes again and thought, *I wouldn't be too sure about that.*

Noah didn't know about that Miss Roxie.

Just as well she'd had to leave for work, he thought on

a suppressed chuckle, as he held the next cabinet steady while Luis bolted it into place, since her carpentry talents were decidedly limited.

Not to mention for a boatload of other reasons. Like the way she'd look at him, so directly it shook him up. Probably every bit as confused as he was, too. Nothing like the coy glances he was used to. Sure, Rox would undoubtedly move mountains if necessary to achieve her own goals—rather than waiting for somebody else to do it for her, which was strangely sexy—but she wasn't the type to pout and whine in order to get her way.

Nag, yes, he thought on another chuckle as he remembered her trying to cajole her uncle into leaving his room by refusing to bring his lunch to him. She'd walked out of the house muttering something about coddling sixty-five-year-old children not being part of her game plan. Except Noah noticed she'd left sandwiches and what all for Charley in the fridge, anyway.

"What's so funny?" Luis asked, repositioning the drill.

"Nothing," Noah said as he checked the level. Dead on. Excellent. "We should have this done by knockoff time, don't you think?"

"Easy," the young man said, hefting the next cabinet into place for Noah to hold. And kind enough to let the subject drop.

Of course, Noah guessed a good part of that directness had to do with her trying to figure him out, too. Or rather, what to do about the chemistry sizzling like acid on metal between them. Whether she'd admit it or not, he had no idea. Whether she'd be amenable to acting on it, he had even less.

Whether *he'd* be amenable to acting on it…now that was the question of the century. And wasn't that a kick in the pants, that there'd even be a question. On his part, anyway.

Because, if she was leaving soon, that was perfect, right? No strings, no ties, no worries about the future....

Yeah. Perfect—if it'd been anybody but Roxie. A thought that made him feel like Luis had taken the drill to his head instead of the wall stud.

The cabinet in place and Luis called away for a minute to help with something else, Noah leaned against the counter and took a swig from the bottle of water he kept refilling from the bathroom sink, the kitchen sink being out of commission until the new laminate counters were installed. Yesterday, when the gal from the other night had called, he hadn't even hesitated to nip the whole thing in the bud. Gently, but firmly. Because somehow, when he hadn't been looking, Roxie had filled up his brain. And until that changed—probably when she left, a prospect that stung far more than it should've—he had no business dating anybody else. Even casually.

Yeah. Go figure.

"Is it safe?" came a gruff voice from a few feet away. He looked over to see Charley standing at the kitchen doorway, back in those crummy coveralls and looking like hell on a bad day, and Noah realized he'd probably never feel safe again, that the earth had shifted underneath his feet and he had no clue what to do about it.

"For the moment. Rox left your lunch in the fridge."

Grunting, Charley slogged across the kitchen, his mouth pulled down at the corners. Noah couldn't resist. "Whatever you broke, I suggest you fix it."

His hand on the refrigerator's handle, the older man swung his head around. "What the hell are you talking about?"

"The fight I'm assuming you and Eden had?"

Another grunt preceded his hauling out the plate of sandwiches, which he then clearly had no idea what to do with, since there were no counters. Noah took the plate from him and carried it out to the dining table, as Charley muttered behind him, "If I'm not gonna talk about it with Rox, I'm sure not gonna talk about it with you. And what do you care anyway?"

"I care because Rox cares," Noah said, which surprised him nearly as much as it apparently did Charley, who came to a dead halt on his way to the table, an expression on his face like Noah'd announced he was from Neptune. "And in any case," Noah continued, once the shock subsided enough to get words out, "*talking about it* is the last thing I want. Do I *look* like a girl?"

That almost got a smile. Or at least, the grooves at the corners of Charley's mouth faded a little. He sank onto the chair where Noah'd set the plate, releasing a gusty sigh before mumbling, "Nobody talks trash about my Rox."

Noah's brows dipped. "What do you mean?"

"Okay, maybe 'trash' is a bit too strong, but..." He wagged his head. "Things kinda went sour, that's all." A bite of sandwich taken, Charley set it back on his plate, the picture of dejection. "But God, I miss her."

"So you *did* break up?"

"I didn't exactly mean to, but...yeah. I guess that's what happened. Rox was right," he said with a curt nod. "I didn't know what I was getting myself into, and now I'm paying for it." He waved Noah away. "You've got stuff to do, you don't need to stick around. I'm lousy company right now, anyway."

If the poor guy hadn't been so obviously heartsick, Noah might've found his drama queen act almost funny.

"Charley?" When Roxie's uncle lifted pain-wracked eyes to his, Noah said, "God knows, I don't claim to know everything about women, but...I've got a little experience with 'em. So if you do want a sounding board? I'm here. Okay?"

"When hell freezes over," Charley said, one side of his mouth barely tilted, "but thanks for the offer."

After a moment, Noah nodded and quietly walked away, although a sizeable chunk of the older man's misery had apparently broken off to follow Noah, doing its level best to find purchase in his gut.

By the time Thursday rolled around, Noah was so tired from pushing through on Charley's house—so he could take on another project waiting in the wings—he'd nearly forgotten that Roxie and her uncle were supposed to come to his parents' that night. Judging from Roxie's voice over the phone, when, after his mother reminded him, he reminded *her,* she'd forgotten as well. Or hoped everyone else would.

"Oh, Lord, Noah…I've finally got Charley downstairs, but actually getting him to leave the house might be a stretch."

"Mom's insisting. In fact…" With one hand propped against the kitchen wall where he was doing the new estimate, he almost winced. "I think she might have someone for him to meet."

"Who? Charley? You're not serious."

"This is my mother we're talking about. Trust me, I'm serious—"

"Who're you talking to?" he heard in the background.

"Noah. Donna and Gene invited us for dinner tonight. I already told him you might not be up for it—"

"What're they having?"

"I have no idea." Then to Noah, as she obviously tried to hold in a laugh, "He wants to know what's on the menu."

"Beats me. Tell him to call Mom if he can't stand the suspense. So, sounds like he's recovering?"

"Apparently so. Although—" she lowered her voice "—he's still being a big old groucheroonie—"

"I heard that! And get off the phone so I can call Donna."

"I'm on my cell, use the landline! Honestly," Roxie said, chuckling aloud by this point. "I guess we'll meet you over there, then. We can't stay long, though, I've got a real early flight to Atlanta tomorrow morning."

A comment that put Noah in a funk for the rest of the day.

She came bearing flowers and candy for his mother, who of course hugged her and told her she shouldn't have— except Noah could tell she was tickled pink, especially about the chocolate—before disappearing back into the kitchen, yelling at Noah to take the gal's coat, for heaven's sake. As if he couldn't figure that one out for himself. Charley immediately followed the sound of ESPN into the family room, where both the big screen TV and Gene resided.

"Mmm…roast pork?" Roxie said as Noah hung up her coat in the closet.

"Yep." Noah turned, fingers shoved in pockets, to admire the way her soft, white, big-collared sweater both clung to her curves and exposed her neck, flanked on either side by long, glittery earrings. "You look good."

"Well, *thank* you," she said, grinning. "Thought I'd wear this to the interview, too. With a skirt, though, not jeans. Opinions?"

"Hey. What I know about fashion can be summed up in three words—*hot* or *not*."

She laughed. "Good enough. And?"

"What do you think?" he said, leaning closer, smelling

her perfume over the rich scent of roasting pig, the combination about to make his head explode, and yep, her eyes darkened and her chest rose…before she took a step backward, craning her neck to see past him.

"So. Where's this chick your mom wants to fix Charley up with?"

Got it. "Not here yet," Noah said. Frustrated. Disappointed. Grateful. "Everyone else is in the living room." A lusty newborn cry pierced the general chaos of a dozen Garretts sharing the same breathing space. "Including little Brady."

Practically shoving him aside, Roxie made a beeline for the living room, where Eli paced, trying to calm the squalling, dark-haired infant. Noah guessed his brother hadn't shaved in several days. Or, judging by the messed up hair and bags under his eyes, slept.

"Where's Tess?" Noah asked over the caterwauling.

"Home. Sleeping," Eli said, jiggling the baby, as his stepdaughter and stepson roared through the living room, Silas's two hot on their heels. He gave a slightly spacey laugh. "She actually fought me about it." He jiggled the baby again; Brady only screamed louder. "Like I couldn't handle my own son for an hour."

Rox lifted her arms. "Give him to me."

Eli shot her an are-you-nuts? look, then nearly dropped the red-faced infant into her arms. "He's fed, changed, burped and pissed about God knows what—"

"Go. Eat. You can come get him when you're done."

"You sure—?"

"We'll be fine." One hand firmly clamped around the little one's back, Rox shooed his daddy away. "Go on. Get."

Sagging with relief and gratitude, Eli blew Rox a kiss before gathering his two charges and heading into the dining room. Noah, however, followed her into the now vacated living room, where she settled with the baby in a corner of the blue-flowered sofa, plopping him on his tummy over her knees and rubbing his back. Almost immediately the infant got a lot quieter, his hollering settling into periodic screeches before, lo and behold, he passed out.

"Okay, that was spooky," Noah said from the doorway.

"Nah, just experience. I used to babysit a lot when I was a teenager. It doesn't always work, of course, but babies pick up on when the person holding them is tense. And poor Eli looks like his brains are leaking out of his ears."

"He's taking this fatherhood thing very seriously. Tess told Mom if she wasn't breastfeeding he might not let her have the baby at all."

Roxie's soft laughter quickly dissolved into an expression that both wrecked and humbled Noah as she shifted the infant to her shoulder and leaned back into the cushions, letting the small, limp body mold to hers. He could practically *feel* her longing, her pain for the baby she'd lost. Except right at that moment she lifted her eyes to his, a slight smile touching her lips.

"Believe it or not, this doesn't make me sad."

"No?"

She shook her head. "More determined, perhaps, to have my own someday. But there's nothing better than the sweet weight of a baby in your arms."

"I know," he said, obviously startling her. "If you hadn't taken him, I would've. Don't know that I could've gotten him to crash like that, but I like holding babies, too."

"As long as you can give them back."

"You got it," he said, telling himself the words sounded hollow because his ears were still ringing from the kid's crying.

"You're a strange one, Noah Garrett." She nuzzled the baby's thick hair, like a shag rug run amok, before contorting her neck to peer down into Brady's squished little face. "I think somebody finally wore himself out."

"You want me to take him so you can eat?"

"No, we're good," she said, slouching farther into the sofa. "You go on. I'm not real hungry, anyway. Too excited about tomorrow. But save me a piece of whatever's for dessert."

"You bet," Noah said, then added, "need a ride to the airport?"

"Oh, thanks...but Charley's taking me. Besides," she said with a little smile, "when I said 'early' I wasn't kidding. I have to leave here at five in order to make it to the airport by six. And I know getting up early isn't your thing."

It could be my thing, he heard inside his head, only to then wonder who'd traded out his brain when he wasn't looking. "Yeah, you're right, that is way too early," he said, and she laughed, grabbing Brady's hands and kissing them when they shot up in his sleep. Noah stood for a moment, stealing one last glance at the pair before heading to the dining room, thinking there was a gal who deserved everything she wanted.

And for damn sure that didn't include him.

"You look like hell," Gene said to Charley as he handed him a can of beer from the minifridge underneath the Garrett's family room bar. Dinner done, the rest of the family had crowded into the living room, knowing better than to encroach on Gene's man cave time.

Grunting, Charley dropped onto the sectional and popped off the top, took a swig. "Could say the same about you. Donna still on your case about working too hard?"

"Does the sun rise in the east?" his friend said with a cross between a sigh and a chuckle, settling into his recliner. "What'd you think of Patty?"

That she's not Edie. "Nice enough gal, I suppose. No spark there, though, to be honest."

"Yeah, that's what I figured. But you know Donna."

"I do that."

They both sipped their beer, idly watching ESPN. Football. Charley hated football, actually, but wouldn't dream of mentioning it. Nor would Gene mention Eden unless Charley did first. That's just the way their friendship worked.

Then Gene shifted in his chair, casting a glance over Charley's head toward the other part of the house before looking at Charley and whispering, "You catch those two with Brady earlier?" and Charley didn't have to ask what Gene was talking about. Because that was another way their friendship worked.

"I certainly did."

"What's your take on it?"

Charley thought a moment, then said, "That youth is definitely wasted on the young."

"Ain't that the truth?" Gene said, settling back again, the beer propped on his stomach. "Can I say something?"

Charley braced himself. "Sure."

"That Roxie of yours turned out to be one fine gal. Smart. Sure of herself. And pretty as they come." His gaze slid to Charley's. "And you know what I think? I think she could work wonders with my boy. That she'd be real good for him. If she'd have him. Don't get me wrong, Noah's a good boy, but he needs some…fine tuning, if you know what I mean." He aimed the remote at the TV to turn up the volume. "Just thought I'd toss that out there."

Charley smiled. "Even though it's none of our business."

"Even though," Gene said with a sly smile. "Even though."

Chapter Eight

On Friday night, her head still in Atlanta—and not in a good way—Roxie and her carry-on trundled blindly down the Albuquerque Sunport concourse toward the meet-and-greet area beyond security, where Charley was supposedly waiting for her. *Supposedly* being the operative word here, she thought as, frowning, she scanned the crowd.

"Rox! Over here!"

And okay, so her heart did a little flippity-flop when she saw Noah instead. Because her heart was an idiot.

As was, apparently, the rest of her, she irritably mused as she watched him shoulder his bad, black-clad self through the mob until he reached her, panting, and irritation instantly morphed to panic.

"Ohmigod—is Charley okay—?"

"What? Yeah, yeah, he's fine. But he got tied up, so he asked if I could meet you instead. Only he didn't call until forty-five minutes ago, and I kept getting your voice mail, so I nearly busted something trying to get here in time—"

At which point her emotions did the lemmings-off-the-cliff thing, and she burst into tears. And launched herself into Noah's arms.

Like she said. *Idiot.*

"Whoa, honey…what happened?"

"I left my phone charger back here," she burbled as he wrapped his arms around her, and she thought, *Okay, so sometimes playing the distraught female has its advantages.* "Along with my pride and common sense."

"You're crying because your phone ran out of juice?"

"No, I…" She weighed the wisdom of what she was about to do, thought, *Screw it, you already threw your sobbing self into his arms, how much worse can it get?* and said, "I need a drink. And food." Then, telling herself to be brave, she pulled out of his arms to wipe her eyes, dig a tissue out of her handbag to blow her nose. "How about dinner?"

"You drink?" This said with a puzzled frown.

"I do now. Well? My treat."

"You're on," he said, which prompted her first laugh in more than twenty-four hours. Soggy though it may have been.

"You don't have a problem with a woman paying your way?"

"Oh, hell no," he said with a chuckle, steering her across miles of tile toward the glass doors, where the crisp night air dried what was left of her tears, blew some of the cobwebs from her brain. "I will, however, probably insist on reciprocating at some point. You okay with that?"

It was scary, how easily she could talk to this guy. Or, in this case, leave tear splotches all over his leather jacket—which smelled really, really good—how at ease she felt with him in so many ways, when in so many other ways they made no sense together.

"I am perfectly okay with that." A moment later they reached his truck in the parking garage and he held the door open for her and helped her in, because it was the biggest-ass truck west of the Mississippi and she was still wearing the stupid straight skirt she'd worn for the interview. And high-heel boots. When she settled into the seat, she noticed he was grinning. She sighed.

"Ogling my butt, were you?"

"It was kinda hard to miss. Because it was right in front of my face," he said, laughing when she shot him a look. And despite her disappointment and borderline humiliation, she was actually very glad to be home.

Inherent complications thereof be damned.

"So. You gonna tell me what went down?" Noah said as they drove, hoping that talking would get his mind off at least some of the crazy, explosive feelings reverberating inside his skull. Partly because he was still digesting what Charley had told him that morning about Roxie, partly because…holding her in his arms? Serious head rush.

She snorted. "Turns out they invited a *dozen* people to interview for the job. In *person*. I mean, they could have at least whittled it down to two or three, right? Because we have this thing called Skype now? But no. Twelve people had to schlep to Atlanta—except for one dude who lived there—for face time."

"Wow. That sucks."

"Tell me about it."

Noah swallowed. "I take it—?" Her eyes cut to his. "Ouch. Obviously not." And was it wrong of him to be not exactly broken up about that? Yes, of course it was. Dumb question. "I'm really sorry, Rox," he said, taking one hand off the wheel to clasp hers. When she sadly shrugged—and held on to his hand, he noticed—he said, "You gonna cry again?"

She seemed to consider this. "Nah. It's *so* nineteenth century. Mostly I'm mad. And feeling really stupid for not finding out what the deal was beforehand." Sighing, she removed her hand. "And what do you mean, Charley was tied up?"

"His words, not mine." Although he could guess. He also figured Rox had enough on her mind without getting into that right now.

Except she jumped right in anyway. "Meaning he's with Eden."

"That would be my take on it, yeah. Unless he's already found someone to replace her."

"Bite your tongue," she muttered, leaning against the passenger side window, only to immediately point to an Italian restaurant coming up on the right. "Oh! Can we eat there? I could devour my weight in shrimp scampi right now."

Noah pulled into the parking lot, taking in the faux Tuscan façade, the courtyard with a fountain. Even he could tell the place wasn't cheap, at least not by Albuquerque standards. "You sure? Might set you back a few bucks."

"You can leave the tip," Roxie said, releasing the seat belt. "How's that?"

"Deal." He got out, going around to help her down from the truck before she fell out and broke something. Except she stumbled anyway, landing smack against his chest. Never one to let an opportunity slip by, Noah hooked his hands on her waist and tugged her closer. "I'm gonna say you don't need that drink."

Rox smirked up at him. "And I'm gonna say you're wr—"

He honest to God hadn't meant to kiss her, but it seemed like a good idea, so he thought *What the hell?* and went for it. Just followed, if not his heart, a couple other things intent on making their preferences heard. And *hel*-lo, damned if she didn't kiss him back, no holds barred, tongue and everything, right there in the halogen-lit parking lot. Kissed him as if this was the last kiss she would ever get. His hands moved from her waist to her jaw, his fingers tangling in those soft, smooth curls as he sank deeper and deeper into something he could feel picking off his brain cells, one by one by one. *Ping. Ping. Pingpingping.*

Eventually, though, common sense tapped his shoulder and cleared its throat, and he let go, only to have her grab the front of his jacket and shake her head. "You have no idea how much I needed that." Then, with a weak laugh, "Heck, *I* had no idea how much I needed that."

"I kinda guessed." He touched his forehead to hers. "Want another one? Because there's a lot more where that came from."

Then he guessed common sense tapped her shoulder, too, because he could see the focus return to her eyes. The truth of the situation. "Oh, you have no idea how much I want another one," she said softly, ruefully, taking his hands in hers. "But—"

He pressed one finger to her lips, even as that *but* walloped him upside the head. "It's okay, you don't have to explain." Stepping away, he curled his hand around hers and tugged her toward the restaurant's entrance. "It never happened, okay?"

Except it had. Because he'd let it. And thanks to following whatever the heck he'd followed he no longer had to wonder what it would be like to kiss her. Now, he knew.

Damn it.

* * *

"You leaving already?"

Buttoning his shirt, Charley looked back at Eden, still in her eyelet-smothered, four-poster bed with the covers pulled up to her chin. Still flushed from fooling around, he thought with a little thrill. Or maybe that was gratitude, that things—his, anyway—still worked. Sitting on the bed, he leaned over and pressed a quick kiss on her coral-smudged lips. "Roxie'll be back soon, she doesn't know I'm here. I don't want her to worry." Then he raised his brows, daring her to say something.

Instead, she sighed and patted his arm. "I wouldn't have called if I wasn't over all that."

"It's not a competition between the two of you—"

"I know, babe. No, really, I do." Clutching the covers, Edie settled farther into the down pillows, surprisingly modest, considering how surprisingly immodest she'd been a little bit ago. "I was just…panicked."

"Why?"

"Because I was scared I'd lose you, what else? So scared I wasn't thinking straight." She smiled. "Swear to God, I won't do it again. Promise."

"Good. Because that nearly killed me."

"Yeah. Me, too."

Edie leaned over and tugged a slithery pink robe off the nearby wing chair, somehow sliding it on without showing anything before getting out of bed, and Charley felt a surge of affection for her so strong it startled him.

They hadn't exactly talked before now, pretty much getting down to business within seconds of his walking in the door an hour earlier, with all the frantic desperation of two lonely souls who'd probably thought they'd never have that kind of connection ever again. Would they be each other's second Great Loves? Charley had no idea. But at this point he was more than willing to settle for close enough. And so, he wagered, was Eden.

"You think Roxie will be okay with this?" she now asked, watching Charley tuck his shirt into his pants, buckle his belt as she finger-combed errant red spikes back into place. Sort of.

"If she's not, she'll simply have to get over it," he said, slipping on his wool sports jacket, pocketing his keys. "Gal's not the boss of me." When, chuckling, Eden sat on the tufted pale blue velvet bench at the foot of the bed, he added, "Besides, I imagine she'll be moving to Atlanta soon, anyway. Once she gets this job."

Eden reached over to take his hand. "You don't exactly sound happy about that."

Charley met her gaze, feeling his forehead pinch. "I don't, do I?"

"Any idea why?"

He thought for a moment. "It's as if I only ever got to borrow her, you know? For a week or two in the summers, that one year she was in high school. These past few months now. I know she was never truly ours—mine—and God knows, she sometimes makes me want to pull out my hair," he said with a rueful half laugh, "but…I'm torn. Between wanting her to do whatever floats her boat and selfishly wanting her to stick around."

A half smile tilted Eden's mouth. "And you know you don't get a vote in it either way, right?"

Charley looked at her for a long moment, then said, "After your husband died, did he ever…talk to you?"

She laughed. "Only all the damn time. Especially in my dreams. Made me nuts. Why? Oh. You, too?"

He crossed his arms. "Yeah. Well, not all the time. And not for a while, actually. But a few weeks ago I got this real clear message that I was supposed to somehow 'fix' Roxie."

"Interesting. Considering the riot act you read me about you two not getting in each other's business."

"I only said I got the message. Not that I'd ever intended to act on it."

"Uh-huh." Her eyes sparkled. "So you sending Noah to pick her up…?"

"Nobody else was available," Charley said, jerking down his sleeve cuff. "He was…convenient."

"Of course he was."

"You don't see them together! The way they interact… he makes her *laugh*, Edie!"

"The maintenance guy here makes me laugh, too. Doesn't mean I want to marry him. Or even schtup him."

"I just thought—"

"Yeah, yeah, I know." She did a "Men, God," eye roll, than stood, clamping her hands around his arms. "Okay. Setting aside your one-eighty about Noah, here's where I throw your own words back in your face. Assuming Roxie's 'broken,' which I'm not all that sure about to begin with, nobody can 'fix' her except Roxie herself. Not you. Not Mae. Not Noah. Or any other man. And whether she goes or stays has nothin' to do with it, either. But considering all the crap she's had to deal with? Hell, she's stronger than you and me put together." She grinned. "Good thing, too, if she's gonna put up with me."

True enough, Charley thought, as a little more of the junk cluttering the inside of his head broke away and floated downstream. Smiling, he kissed the top of Eden's head before opening her door. Then he turned and said, "You know…I think you and I could be very good together."

Her eyes shimmered. "Funny. I was thinking the same thing," she said, and he could have *sworn* he heard Mae heave out a relieved sigh. Or maybe it was only the wind, pushing through the open door.

Charley kissed Edie again, then left, whistling quite the merry little tune as he walked down the stairs and out to his car.

Roxie's head was still buzzing as she climbed the steps to the house after Noah dropped her off. Without, it should be noted, any more hanky-panky, as if they'd come to some sort of mutual unspoken agreement that as far as bad ideas went? That was the granddaddy of them all.

Never mind the electricity arcing between them during dinner, even as they pretended the kissy-face session out in the parking lot had never happened. Although she had to say, the necking definitely took the edge off losing the job. Or maybe that was the two glasses of pinot blanc with dinner. Or maybe the wine had taken the edge off knowing she would never, ever, ever kiss Noah again. Ever.

Okay, now she was making herself depressed.

She let herself inside, to find a humming Charley reloading cabinets in the newly finished kitchen, now a symphony in tans and creams and blacks. Pretty. If they'd had a kitchen table she would have definitely sat at it, since, between the flight and unwinding and the kissing and the wine she wasn't entirely sure how long she had until her knees gave out. Not to mention her brain. Which finally caught up to Charley's humming.

Ah.

"Let me guess. You and Eden are back together."

A stack of bread plates in his hands, Charley grinned over at her. "We are. At least we're going to give this thing between us a real shot, see where it goes." Then the grin melted into a frown. "You okay with that?"

"Of course," Roxie said gamely. "If she really makes you happy—"

"When we're not arguing?" The plates clattered onto the shelf. "Yeah. She does."

Okay, then. Charley had charged ahead with his life. Good for him. And God willing, the woman wouldn't drive him insane, or break his heart, or take him for every penny he had. But, hey—life was all about taking risks, right?

"And this way," he added, clunking another stack of plates on the shelf, "you don't have to worry about me being alone once you leave."

"Not an issue," she said on a sigh. Yep, Charley was striking out for distant shores, and here she was, treading water. "Not yet, anyway."

Brows drawn, Charley met her gaze again. "You didn't get the job?"

"No." She made do with the old step stool, now looking woefully out of place amidst all the Gleaming and New. "It's okay," she said with a wave of her hand, even though, now that the wine and the endorphins were wearing off, it wasn't. Drat. "The Atlanta traffic sucks anyway."

"I'm sorry, kiddo—"

"I *said*, it's okay. Any mail come while I was gone?"

"Over there, on the counter. Which looks great, by the way. It all does. Now that it's done, I'm glad you forced me into it."

"You're not just saying that?" she said, spotting the Priority Mail envelope with Jeff's return address.

"When have you ever known me to blow air up anybody's skirt? No. The old kitchen looked like Mae. This looks like me."

Never mind that he hadn't chosen so much as the paint color, Roxie thought with a half smile as she slit open the envelope, letting a half dozen CDs she had no interest in listening to, ever again, clatter onto the new laminate. To her consternation, her eyes burned, even though she knew beyond a doubt she'd been over Jeff for months. This wasn't the numbness of denial, either, but the relief of simply no longer caring.

The emotional betrayal, though, combined with lingering self-condemnation for thinking she could simply transfer all her hopes and dreams from Mac to Jeff, like switching out a bank account—that she wasn't over nearly as much as she might have thought. Or wished.

And her reaction to Noah's kisses tonight only reinforced that.

Because let's be clear, boys and girls—girlfriend was needy as hell. Emotionally, physically, the lot. But tumbling into bed with Noah—and she had no doubt the option was on the table, should she be inclined to exercise it—would solve nothing. Not for her, anyway. And right now? It was all about doing—or, in this case, not doing—what was best for her. And what was best for her was sticking to what was safe. What made sense.

And Noah didn't fit either of those criteria. At all.

Moving on. Great idea in theory, not so easy in practice.

Although Noah had worked some at Charley's that Saturday to keep the momentum going, he'd only seen Roxie briefly as he was leaving and she was getting home from the clinic. They exchanged pleasantries, he caught her up on the progress, she caught him up on Charley and Eden, they said good-night and that was that. It hadn't seemed prudent to mention he'd slept for crap the night before, having no idea at the time he wouldn't sleep for crap that night or the one following, either.

So here he was on Monday, sleep-deprived as all hell,

albeit conscious enough—barely—to realize he'd never lost sleep over a woman before. Granted, he thought as he watched her turn the dining table into her own branch of Ship 'n' Check, there was an outside chance he could chalk it all up to plain old sexual frustration. Meaning there was also an outside chance if they'd just get it on, already, he'd be able to sleep again. And yes, if Roxie could read minds he'd be dead right now.

Naturally she picked that moment to look up, frowning, and damned if his face didn't get hot. She picked up a packing tape dispenser, slapping it against a box. "You need me for anything?"

She should only know. With the morning light teasing her dark hair, her neck where she'd pulled it up save for a bunch of little corkscrew curls around her temples, she looked nearly edible. "Just wondering what you're doing."

Roxie jerked the tape across the package. "Packing up Mae's stuff that sold on eBay so Charley won't have to worry about it. If necessary, I'll come back in the spring, hold a sale for whatever's left over."

Noah's stomach dropped. "You found a job?"

Her mouth twisted. "I wish. But you know me, ever the optimist. Obviously, if I'm still here..." He saw her chest rise with her breath. "Anyway." She rubbed her hands down the sides of her sweatshirt. "So you guys are almost finished?"

"Hope to be done and gone by Wednesday, yep."

"Charley's really pleased," she said, wrapping tissue, then bubble wrap, around a figurine of some kind. "But then he's floating on cloud nine these days, anyway. Did I tell you? He and I are going to Eden's for Thanksgiving."

"No. That should be...interesting."

"There's one word for it," she said with a low, just-Rox-being-Rox laugh, and Noah thought, *It's not gonna be the same when you're gone—*

"Noah? I know you're here, son, your truck's outside."

Roxie's head jerked up. "Your dad?"

"Yep. Said he might stop by sometime today, see how things were going."

"Checking up on you, you mean?" she whispered. "Man, that is *so* bogus."

Noah blinked at her, not sure whether to be more amused by her skateboard-dude-speak or flummoxed by her immediate defense. Flummoxed, and oddly…pleased. Gratified. Turned on. "It's okay," he mouthed, leaving the room to meet his father in the foyer.

And even more oddly, it was. Because at some point he'd concluded that, actually, he didn't need to prove a blamed thing to his father. Or anybody else. He was hardworking, reliable and good at what he did. If his dad couldn't see that, it was his problem. Not Noah's.

Gene was already in the kitchen inspecting the cabinets, eyeballing the countertop levels, squinting at the tile floors. Arms crossed, Noah leaned against the doorjamb, watching, catching Roxie's scent as she came up behind him. His fierce little wingman, he thought with a funny twist to his midsection.

"Looks okay," Gene said, high praise for him. Only before Noah could get out his thanks, Roxie squirmed past him.

"It's a lot more than *okay*, Mr. Garrett," she said, a smile in her voice.

"Rox—"

"Hey." She wheeled on Noah, puffed up like a little bantam hen. And although she was smiling, she definitely had a *fear-me* glint in her eyes. "Am I the customer, or what? So you just hush and let me say my piece." Then she spun back to his dad. "'Okay,' my butt. It's *fantastic*. And he's ahead of schedule *and* coming in under budget."

Startled, Gene looked from Roxie to Noah—who, not about to take offense at her defense, simply shrugged— then back to Roxie. "You don't say?" his dad said, his eyes twinkling. "Well, if you're satisfied—"

"Try *thrilled*."

"Then so am I," his father said with a slight bow. "Although I take it you don't mind if I check up on some of the technical things?"

"Go right ahead. Although I can't imagine you'll find any problems."

Despite choking back a laugh, Noah was sorely tempted to pick the gal up by the back of her sweatshirt and remove her from the room before things got any more embarrassing. Especially when his father said, "Maybe you should let me be the judge of that?"

"Sure, do what you gotta do," she said with a flick of her hand, and marched out of the room, leaving Noah alone with his father. And a whole boatload of speculation, he'd wager.

"Sounds like you've got a real fan there," Gene said casually, after they'd toured the rest of the house, checking the repairs to the windows and floors before moving outside to the porch, which, under Noah's supervision, his brothers had repaired and repainted.

"Completely unsolicited, I swear."

His father let out a low chuckle. "Gal reminds me a lot of your mother when we were first dating."

"You're kidding?"

"Nope. Her passion, her honesty. Her fearlessness…" Looking over at his own house, Gene shrugged. "I remember thinking, when we first met, we'd probably knock heads at least once a day, but I'd never be bored. And I was right."

He grinned. "On both counts. I never know what's gonna come out of that woman's mouth. Probably why we've never run out of things to talk about." He paused, then said, "She also told me I needed to stop being an old stick in the mud and trust you more. With the business, I mean. And on the surface, I agree with her."

"Finally," Noah muttered, but his father's hand shot up.

"Not so fast." Leaning his backside against the porch railing, he folded his arm over his heavy plaid jacket. "I'm still not exactly on board with some of your lifestyle choices."

Noah's eyes met his father's. "And I can't seriously believe you're going down this road again."

Gene's shoulders hitched. "Don't get me wrong, the house looks good. Real good. I've got no complaints about your work. But image counts for a lot more than we sometimes want to believe, whether we like it or not. How a person conducts himself carries every bit as much weight as how well he does his job. I know I can't make you into somebody you're not. That I've got no right to ask you to change, but—"

"Then stop trying," Noah said softly, his gaze swinging across the street.

"I can't help it. Just like I can't help that people naturally trust family men more. That's simply human nature, I didn't make it up—"

"Dad. For crying out loud..." On a strained half laugh, Noah faced Gene again. "You say that like being married is some sort of vaccination against never doing anything wrong again. Have you *listened* to the news lately? Plenty of married men screw up—"

"Not Garretts," his father said, as if it was an indisputable fact, then walked over to clap Noah's shoulder. "And sometimes a parent feels obligated, for his kid's own good, to point out things he knows the kid doesn't want to hear. Believe me, it would be much easier to keep my mouth shut. Except when you want that kid to be the best he can be? You don't." Gene squeezed his arm again, then started down the steps, leaving Noah to gag on the stench of his father's continued disapproval.

Despite his determination not to let the old man get to him, his stomach churned like a disturbed riverbed as he watched Gene walk out to his truck. Several deep breaths later he walked back inside to find Roxie in the living room, another box of Mae's stuff clamped in her hands and her eyes so full of sympathy he wanted to barf.

"You were eavesdropping?"

"You bet," she said mildly, setting the box on top of several others by the front door.

Anger exploded in his gut. "Coming to my defense earlier was one thing, even if it was totally unnecessary. But to blatantly listen in on a conversation that has nothing to do with you—"

"Was wrong and rotten and bad. I know." She straightened, facing him. And not the least bit repentant. "But at least it saves you the trouble of filling me in when you get over yourself enough to properly bitch about it."

"And what makes you think I need to do that?"

"Maybe because you look like you could snap nails in two with your teeth right now?"

"I'm fine."

"Bull."

Noah looked at her for a long moment, then wheeled and strode out of the room, hoping she'd get the message, that he wanted to be left alone, dammit. But no, she had to trail him like a hound dog through the house and outside to the backyard, where he slammed the palm of his hand against the trunk of an enormous, bare-limbed ash. He heard the dry grass crunch as she approached, stopping a good six or so feet away.

"For what it's worth?" she said. "You handled that with a helluva lot more restraint than I would have. That was seriously impressive."

"You're not going away, are you?"

"Nope. Just like you didn't go away the night of the pizza party. So deal. And by the way? Not sure I appreciate being made a substitute target, either."

A reluctant smile pushing at his mouth, Noah dropped his hand. Faced her. "I'd honestly thought I didn't care anymore. What he thought."

"I know," Rox said gently, and the irritation twisted into something far worse, something he had no idea how to handle. "And I swear I didn't mean to make you more angry. But I was so angry *for* you I couldn't help it." She shrugged. "Like I said. No restraint."

Right. This from the woman who had consciously chosen not to be bitter about the hand—hands—fate had dealt her. Then it registered what she'd said. "You don't agree with Dad?"

"Well," she said, perching awkwardly on the arm of an old, peeling Adirondack chair planted in the middle of the yard, "the part about people's skewed perceptions?" She let out an aggravated sigh. "Unfortunately, that's pretty much true." Snorting, Noah looked away. "But that doesn't mean I don't understand your frustration. Your crew obviously respects you. Hell, from what I can tell, they flat out worship you. Why your father can't see that, can't accept… *you*…"

He turned back to find her gripping the arm of the chair so tightly her hands looked like claws. "Ohmigod, it makes me so mad I could spit! To…to follow tradition simply because that's the way it's always been done? Especially about something as monumental as getting married? Having kids? Who gets to decide this stuff?"

Okay, color him slightly confused. "But…you're totally down with the whole marriage and kids thing."

"For *me*, yeah," Rox said, nearly toppling over when she pressed one hand to her chest. "Not for everybody. And to use marriage as some sort of yardstick to measure somebody's integrity…I can't even wrap my head around that, sorry. You have a right to live your own life, Noah, the way *you* want to live it. Not the way your father wants you to. So there."

Wow. Then, realizing she was shivering because she was probably freezing, Noah slipped out of his jacket and handed it to her, feeling another one of those funny gut twists when she practically disappeared inside it. "Thanks," she said.

Noah nodded, then smiled slightly. "Looks like there's no reason for me to bitch. Seeing as you already did it for me."

A stray, still-yellow leaf rappelled through the mostly bare branches to land in Roxie's lap. Idly, she picked it up, talking almost more to it than to him.

"Yeah, well, it hit home. See, apparently my parents had plans for me. Plans that didn't include me making a career out of telling people how much Great-Aunt Edna's eighteenth-century armoire was worth. Especially since my father had done the struggling artist thing most of their married life. Meaning Charley and Mae weren't exactly encouraging, either. We fought," she said to his questioning gaze. "A lot. Hence the Goth phase. And why I put myself through college. Out of state. That's also why I didn't come back very often to see them, because we'd get into the same argument every time I did. And it hurt, because I loved them. But it seemed the only way to ensure their happiness was to sacrifice my own."

Huh. Maybe they had more in common than he'd thought. "What did your parents want you to do?"

She smirked. "Anything that was 'stable.' As if such a thing exists in today's economy, anyway. Except maybe working for the IRS or going into undertaking," she said dryly. "They all meant well. I even knew it at the time. But we can't be who other people want us to be. Not successfully anyway." The fire flared again in her eyes. "God knows, your dad's a good man. But so are you. And it chaps my hide that he can't see that because his definition doesn't jibe with yours."

And again, her defense warmed him. However…"Rox—my reputation…that's not rumor, you know."

"Being a chick magnet doesn't automatically make you a dirtwad."

At that, he laughed out loud. "Oh, honey…if I was ever in a back alley fight? I'd definitely want you on my side."

Her eyes locked in his, she huddled more deeply into his jacket. "Same here," she said.

Then Noah said, "You're treading on real thin ice, you know that?" and her brows lifted.

"What's that supposed to mean?"

"That you have no idea how badly I want to kiss you again."

"Never mind that two minutes ago you were mad at me."

"Which would be two minutes before you blew my mind."

Then it seemed as if another two minutes passed before, on a rush of air, she said, "Okay, here's the thing—you have no idea how much I'd like to kiss you again, too—no, stay where you are, I'm not finished—but the problem is, kissing has a way of leading to other things. Which in theory is very nice. In fact, I'm a real big fan of 'other things,' but, see…I learned the hard way that I'm not one of those women who can fool around and then go about my merry way. I…bond. Big time."

"As in…?"

"As in, my hormones turn to Super Glue and you'll never get rid of me. Well, not without the words 'twenty-to-life' being in there somewhere. And I'm thinking that's not what you have in mind."

"Going to prison?"

Rox laughed, then sobered, a smile still lingering on her lips. "I refuse to be anybody's jailer, Noah. Ever again. Please don't think I'm only being a tease," she said, concern swimming in her eyes, "because that's not my intention. But I know who I am, what I want and need. I don't have to defend it or make excuses for it, but I do have to honor it. Honor myself. And I have to honor you, too, by not letting you get into something you don't want."

"But—"

"Sex isn't a momentary thing for me. It's a commitment. And yes, I know that makes me an oddball in this day and age, but that's my cross to bear. So I'm going to save both of us a lot of grief and say the subject is now off the table."

He felt almost dizzy. "Forever?"

She got to her feet, letting his jacket slide off her arms before she handed it back to him. "Maybe we could make each other feel good for a little while," she said, and Noah thought, *Maybe, hell,* "but we wouldn't make each other happy. And making do simply isn't enough anymore. Not for me."

"You're still not over…what was his name? Mac?"

Instead of answering, she simply gave him one of those inscrutable smiles before walking back to the house.

Swallowing hard, Noah realized he couldn't argue with her, or rise to her unspoken challenge to make her *forget* her first love. That she'd been absolutely right to walk away. That he should be grateful she'd refused to compromise his freedom.

Except, somehow he didn't think "freedom" was supposed to leave such a sour taste in your mouth.

Chapter Nine

God help her, Roxie thought on Thanksgiving Day, as she listened to Charley and Eden trade good-natured barbs across the table from each other, the woman was beginning to grow on her. In much the same way one did get sucked into all those absurd reality shows, actually. Eccentric didn't even begin to cover it, she further mused when Eden bounced up from the table, one of her custom-made creations billowing around her as she floated to the kitchen to warm up the gravy, her prissy little dog clickity-clicking behind her. But she was clearly as smitten with Charley as he was with her, and jeezum, could the woman cook. So things could be a lot worse.

"So the house is all finished?" Eden now asked, settling back at the table like a swan on her nest.

Ah, yes. That. If nothing else, being here—up until this moment, at least—had diverted Roxie from thinking too hard about that last conversation with Noah. About the slightly horrified look in his eyes when she'd laid down what must have sounded like an ultimatum.

When she'd deliberately not answered that last question. Because right now, it was all about tossing out whatever obstacles came to hand, anything to slow down this runaway *thing* exploding between them.

"It sure is," Charley said, chest expanded as if he'd done all the work himself. "And it looks terrific." Then he smiled at Roxie. "Thanks to your nagging, girl."

"Noah and his crew really did a great job," she said, poking holes in her yams, fascinated with the marshmallow ooze. Then, smiling for Eden, "You really need to come see the house."

Setting down her wine glass, the other woman eyed her speculatively. "You sure?"

Roxie reached out and took Eden's hand, clearly startling her. "Absolutely. You're welcome anytime." Letting go, she raised her own glass to her uncle and grinned. "Anything to get this old coot off my back!"

Eden barked out a laugh, then took up her knife and fork to resume her demolition of her turkey leg. "I like you, honey." She waved her knife in Roxie's direction. "You've got brass ones, doncha?"

Do I? she thought. Because if that were true, would she cut herself off from something she wanted so badly it made her cross-eyed, simply because she wasn't sure she could handle the aftermath?

Across the room, her phone warbled. "Sorry," she said, scooting over to get it out of her purse. "I can't imagine who it is...."

Seeing Noah's number on the readout sent a jolt through her midsection. "Noah—?"

"I'm sorry, I must be interrupting your dinner—"

"No, no, not a problem." Frowning, she shoved her hair behind her ear. "What's going on?"

She heard a rattling sigh. "Dad…he had a heart attack."

"Ohmigod, Noah! Is Gene…is he okay?"

"He's out of recovery after the angioplasty. So I guess so far, so good. He's still a little groggy, but definitely conscious. And a helluva lot calmer than the rest of us," he said with the tense laugh of the petrified. "And…he asked to see you."

Something close to alarm wrapped its long, bony fingers around her neck. And squeezed. "Me? Why?"

"You'd have to ask him that. So. Will you come?"

"Of course," Roxie said, quickly, before the galloping heart rate, the cold, sick feeling in the pit of her stomach, had a chance to fully register. After Noah told her which hospital, she elbowed aside the panic enough to ask, "Hey… how are *you* doing?"

"Better now than I was a few hours ago," he said on another shaky laugh that made her ache for him, and the panic ebbed…only to rush her from another, even more vulnerable angle, that she could deny it 'til the cows came home, but the fact was—big sigh, here—she was completely, hopelessly, pointlessly in love with the doofus.

"And your mom?" she said over the burning sensation in her eyes.

"A basket case in denial?"

"I bet," she said, then swallowed. "I'll be there in five minutes. What's the room number?"

She found a pen in a drawer, scribbled the number on a paper towel, then turned to find that Eden and Charley had already put everything away and were in their coats, ready to go, worry heavy in Charley's eyes as he held Eden's hand.

Slipping into her coat, Roxie grabbed for her uncle's

other hand. "Hey. This is Gene we're talking about. He's going to be fine."

Probably a lot better than I am, Roxie thought on a sigh, as she herded the couple out to her car.

It took longer to navigate the hospital's endless corridors than it had to get there from Eden's, although the interminable marching at least gave her a chance to come to terms with her surroundings. To pat herself on the back that she hadn't walked through the glass doors, said, "Nope, can't do this," and gone tearing back out to the parking lot, a hyperventilating blur in an ivory mohair swing coat.

But she didn't. And at long last, Roxie and her mini-entourage found the coronary care waiting room, filled cheek-by-jowl with Garretts. Noah stood immediately, shaking hands with Charley and nodding to Eden before yanking Roxie against him and holding on tight. With his brothers watching, heh. But—and here was the weird thing—almost as if he were comforting *her*.

When he finally let go, searching her eyes for heaven knew what, she said, "Where's your mom?"

"In with Dad. The doctor came out a little bit ago, said if everything kept on as expected, Dad should only be in the hospital a day or so. But he's gonna be fit to be tied when the sedation wears off completely." He took her slightly aside, saying through a thick voice, "For all the man and I don't see eye to eye, I can't…"

"I know," she said, laying her hand on his arm. "I know."

At that moment, Donna Garrett emerged from the room, looking a little wan but collected—enough—in her Thanksgiving getup of a long, leaf-patterned skirt, a sweatshirt with gleefully oblivious turkeys marching across the yoke. Her sons all stood; she waved them back down. Seeing Roxie, she managed a smile, the skirt whooshing around her thighs when she sank onto the nearest seat, the adrenaline rapidly waning. She rallied enough, though, to give Charley a hug when he leaned over.

"He's dozing," she said to the room at large as she smoothed back her flyaway hair, then sagged back against the vinyl cushion, her eyes drifting closed. "He may have been the one who had the heart attack, but mine will never be the same, let me tell you." Then she opened her eyes and spotted Roxie. "Oh, my goodness…you came?"

"Well, yeah, of course." Roxie sat beside her, hugging her purse to her middle. "Because Noah said Gene asked for me?"

"About a half hour ago." Reaching for Roxie's hand, Donna gave her a gentle smile. "He wouldn't tell anybody why, but he was pretty insistent. Fair warning, though, honey—he was still pretty doped up at that point. He might not even remember asking. Hate to think you came all the way up here on a fool's errand."

"No, actually, I was already here, having dinner with Eden. But I would've come no matter what." Then, remembering her manners, Roxie introduced Eden to everyone… a moment before, unfurling her voluminous shawl, Eden plunked herself down on Donna's other side.

"I know we just met, so forgive my butting in…but I've got a pretty good idea what you're feeling right now—"

"Oh, I'll be fine in a minute—"

"Like hell." Tears glistened in Eden's mascara. "You might be brave. You might even be calm. But *fine?* No damn way. Trust me, sweetheart, I've been there. I know. Just like I know you need to let it out. And far better in front of me than your husband, right?"

Roxie could see Donna's valiant fight to hold it in—the tiny shake of her head, the tight press of her lips. But then, on a long, soft moan, she dissolved into tears, not even protesting when Eden pulled Noah's mother against her chest, making soft, crooning noises of her own.

Holy cow.

Suddenly overcome with all the emotions she'd thought she'd left back in the parking lot, Roxie stood and fled into the hall, only to hear Noah's soft, "Bringing back memories?" behind her seconds later.

She jerked around. "How did you—? Oh. You mean about the baby?"

He came closer. Wearing a brown T-shirt underneath a tan denim jacket, she noticed. Not black. "Well, that, too. But a couple of days ago, while you were at work? Charley got to talking." Compassion flooded his eyes. "Said you were at the hospital with your parents after the crash. By yourself."

Unable to speak for the tears clogging her throat, Roxie simply nodded. A second later she was once more in Noah's arms, his head nestled atop hers. "I can't imagine how awful that was for you," he whispered. "And then…the other."

"Yeah. Not a big fan of hospitals," she finally got out, pulling away. But he grabbed her hand.

"Maybe I had to tell you Dad wanted to see you, but you didn't have to say yes."

"I know. But I would've come in any case." She took a deep breath, thinking, *Fear is for wusses.* "Even if you'd only asked for yourself."

His brows lifted. "Really?"

"Really. So why didn't you?"

Still holding her hand, Noah glanced down, pushing out a sigh before meeting her gaze again. "Because I can't figure out what we are to each other. And whether whatever that is includes being able to call on you in a crisis."

"Don't make me smack you," Roxie said, and he smiled.

"Look, I don't know what we are to each other, either. But I sure as heck know I hate it when we're not talking."

He gave her a crooked smile. "Me, too—"

"Rox?" Silas said from the waiting room doorway. "The nurse said Gene's asking for you."

Noah walked her to his father's door, giving her hand a brief squeeze before returning to the waiting room. But oh, dear God—the déjà vu when she stepped inside, saw Gene hooked up to all those whirring and beeping machines, was so strong she had to force herself to breathe.

Her father had passed away in the E.R. within minutes after being brought in, but her mother had hung on for almost another full day, although she never regained consciousness. Mae and Charley had gotten there as soon as they could, but Charley had told Noah the truth, that all through that long, horrible night she'd been by herself, barely seventeen and frightened out of her wits, staving off the agony of losing her father by willing her mother to stay alive. How she'd ever recovered from that, she'd never know. Let alone gone on to recover from Mac's death, from losing the baby, from Jeff's betrayal....

Noah was right, she thought with a slight smile. She was one tough little cookie.

Fortunately, Noah's dad didn't appear to be going anywhere, thank God, even though he was still a bit loopy from the meds. But his color looked pretty good, from what she could tell, and the machines all seemed to be beeping and whirring as they should.

At Gene's indication that she should sit, Roxie silently lowered herself onto the edge of the padded chair next to the bed. "How do you feel?"

He almost smiled. "I'm gonna say like crap, although I'm not entirely sure."

"I bet." She swallowed. "You...wanted to see me?"

Gene rolled his head to look at her, grimacing at the oxygen tube in his nose. "It's funny," he said slowly. "In the back of your mind you know you don't have forever, but even further back you think you do. The doc says I'm gonna make it, but I'm not taking any chances. You sweet on my boy?"

Nothing like cutting to the chase. "Oh, Gene…if this is going where I think you're taking it…please don't—"

"I'm only asking 'cause I know he's got feelings for you." He pulled in a noisy breath. "Strong feelings. Stronger than he's probably ever had for anyone else his entire life. So before I make a damn fool of myself, I need to know if those feelings are reciprocated."

Damn. Damndamndamndamndamn. What on earth was she supposed to say? Maybe the man wasn't dying, but he wasn't exactly in optimal health, either.

"Okay, forget that," Gene said, and Roxie puffed out a sigh of relief, only to nearly choke when he said, "I'm gonna say my piece, anyway. If anybody could help that boy get his head on straight, it's you. He *needs* you, honey. Even if he's too mule-headed to see it, I do."

"Gene—"

"I know, I know…his past doesn't exactly speak in his favor. But he's right on the cusp of changing, I can feel it. And I believe that's because of you. So if you could find it in your heart to give him a little encouragement…?"

The privacy curtain yanked back. "Okay, Mr. Garrett," said the broad-hipped, broadly smiling nurse. "We don't want you overexerting yourself now, do we?"

"But we weren't finished—"

"And there's no hurry, honey, I promise. Everything's looking good. No reason on earth why you can't continue this tomorrow when you're feeling stronger." She smiled down at Roxie. "You got a problem with waiting?"

"Me?" She practically shot to her feet. "Not at all. You have a nice, quiet night, Gene," she said, leaning over to kiss his forehead, "and…I'll see you soon, how's that—?"

He clasped her hand. "You'll think about what I said?"

As if she was going to be able to think about anything else. "I will. I promise."

"And you won't say anything to Noah?"

"He knows you asked to see me. Don't you think he's going to be the tiniest bit curious as to why?"

The nurse shot her a let's-not-upset-the-cardiac-patient-okay? look, and Roxie sighed. "I promise, I won't say anything to Noah. Do you want me to send Donna or the boys back in?"

"Donna. Please."

Naturally, Noah immediately jerked to attention when she came out of the room. Her brain going a mile a minute, Roxie delivered the message to Donna, then walked a little apart from the others, figuring Noah would follow.

"The nurse shooed me out before he could say very much. And he wasn't making a whole lot of sense, really." Which was true enough. "Although…" She looked up at him. "I think maybe this experience has made him think differently about you."

"What's that supposed to mean? And why tell you?"

"I have no idea, and I don't think this is the best time to look for logic."

He exhaled. "No. I guess not."

Searching for an excuse to leave, to give herself space to figure out what the heck to do about this responsibility Gene had dumped on her, Roxie spotted her uncle and Eden. "I hate to do this, but there's no real reason for Charley and Eden to stay, and I drove them here. So if it's all the same to you…"

"No, no, that's okay. We're going to try to get Mom to go

home in a little while," Noah said with a small, tired smile, "although nobody's holding their breath on how well that's gonna work. But thanks for coming. I'm sure it meant a lot to Dad." He rubbed his mouth, then crossed his arms. "And to me."

Roxie stood on tiptoe to kiss his cheek, breathing in his scent, which ignited a sweet ohmigod-I-wanna-make-babies-with-this-man ache in the center of her chest, and she thought, *Biology blows.* "Tell your mom if she needs anything, anything at all, I'm right across the street." *For now, at least.* "And call me when you get home. Anytime, even if it's late," she said.

He said, "Okay," even though she knew he wouldn't.

"Nothing more to do here, let's go home," she said, waving Eden and Charley over, ignoring their puzzled expressions as best she could as she said goodbye to the rest of the Garretts and started down the hall toward the elevators, Noah's questioning gaze burning a hole in her back the entire way.

Fortunately—deliberately?—once back in the car, Eden dragged Charley into a conversation about old movies Roxie couldn't even begin to take part in, followed by her uncle's dozing off almost immediately after they dropped Eden back at her place.

Leaving Roxie with nothing but tacky arrangements of Christmas carols on the car radio and her own thoughts to keep her company as she drove.

Blech.

"Charley? Charley!" she said after pulling up into his driveway some time later.

"Wh— Huh?" Her uncle jerked awake, blinking like a sedated owl.

"We're home."

Well, *he* was anyway, Roxie mused as she pulled her

phone out of her purse, halfheartedly checking her Face-book page while keeping an eye on her drowsy uncle as they climbed the steps. Because hell if she knew where her home was.

Oh, joy, a friend request. Probably some friend of a friend of a friend she'd never met in her life. Yawning, she clicked on the icon, only to let out a shriek of delight when a very familiar face popped up on the tiny screen.

It was well after midnight before Noah and his brothers finally convinced their mother to go home, get some rest, they'd bring her back as early as she wanted in the morning. Meaning, by that point, he wasn't about to call Roxie. A good thing, all told, since he wanted to hear her voice way too much.

By the next morning, though, when they'd all trooped into Dad's room to find him sitting up and eating oatmeal and fake eggs—and moaning and groaning about it the en-tire time—yesterday's scare already felt like a bad dream... leaving a new reality in its wake. Because even if Dad took care of himself, lost some weight, exercised more, he couldn't keep driving himself the way he'd been.

Amazingly, Gene was the first one to admit that life as they'd all known it was never going to be the same. "I'm glad you're all here, because we need to talk about the future—"

"Dad," Silas said, his eyes bleary behind his glasses. "This can wait for five minutes."

"No, it can't. Because if you all want me to rest easy, then I need to have this settled in my head." As Donna, seated beside the bed, wrapped her hand around their fa-ther's, his eyes landed on Noah. "Well, son...you wanted more responsibility? You got it. From here on out, you're in charge."

Noah flinched. "Excuse me?"

"You heard me. You're the boss."

"What? No...the doctor said you'd probably be back at work in a week—"

"I know. But I made a promise to your mother, even after the docs give me the all clear, to cut my involvement way back. Oh, I'll still keep a hand in, retirement would drive me insane—and her, too, even if she won't admit it—but I'm turning the day-to-day stuff over to you."

Stunned, Noah looked at Eli and Jesse, standing in almost identical, arms-crossed poses at the foot of the bed. "But you guys—"

"Come January, I'm going back to school, remember?" Jesse said, his pushed-up hoodie sleeves revealing almost solidly tattooed arms. "So I'll only be around part-time."

"And with the baby," Eli said, "I'm already behind in furniture orders as it is. I can't possibly catch up and oversee everything else."

"Besides," Gene put in, "you're right. Nobody knows the business like you do. So—it's yours. Since we're closed until Monday, anyway, we can work out the details after I get home."

Noah could imagine what some of those "details" might be. "That's...it?" he asked. Prodding. "No stipulations?"

His father regarded him in silence for a moment, then said, "Only that you remember whose standard you're bearing. And that I have the right to change my mind at any time."

"Like hell," their mother muttered, earning her a chorus of soft laughs.

"I won't let you down," Noah said.

"And I'm counting on you to keep that promise," Gene said, and Noah could still see flickers of doubt in his eyes, that while Noah may have been his only choice, he still wasn't necessarily his best.

Then his brothers said their goodbyes, with promises to stop by later, before easing back into their own lives. Their own brands of crazy. Noah was the last to give hugs, the last out of the room. And as he stopped by a water fountain to get a drink, he wondered...what did *he* have, besides new, hard-won responsibilities that came with enough entailments to sink a battleship? A sink devoid of female clutter? Nights uninterrupted by an infant's cry? The satisfaction of knowing that when he sat down to watch a movie he'd actually get to finish it?

That so-called "freedom?"

At which point, a thought that had been poking and prodding and trying to find a way into his brain showed its face in a dingy window, waving like mad to get his attention, its voice faint but insistent.

"Hey, bro," Silas said as they all piled into the elevator. "You okay?"

"Yeah, of course. Why wouldn't I be?"

Silas and Eli exchanged a glance before Eli said, "You don't exactly look happy about that conversation. Even though you've been after Dad for years to give you more authority."

"Because I'd always pictured that happening because he wanted to," he ground out. "Not because he didn't have a choice!"

The conversation died a quick death when a yakking family of five piled onto the elevator on the next floor...and when they all got off Noah strode away from his brothers, hopefully sending a clear message that he was in no mood to pick it up again. Not that they wouldn't at some point, but right now all he wanted was to be by himself.

Which wasn't exactly true, he thought, as he started

back to Tierra Rosa. Right now, all he wanted was to hang out with Roxie. To somehow absorb some of that level-headedness, to hear her laughter. So when he noticed her car clinging like a mountain goat to Charley's steep drive-way as he drove past, a nice little inner battle ensued as he reminded himself that what *he* wanted wasn't fair to her, that it was self-centered and childish.

And that he was better than that.

Except no sooner had he passed than he remembered it was the day after Thanksgiving. Meaning, in Garrett-ville, the day the Christmas decorations went up—his mom decked the halls from top to bottom, while his dad set up an outside display easily rivaling the Chevy Chase *Christmas Vacation* movie. Which, Noah thought as his eyes stung, along with *Muppets' Christmas Carol* and *It's a Wonderful Life*, they'd all watched every year.

His gut clenched. Because suddenly, he felt like a planet jettisoned from orbit, flung far, far away from its solar system.

Like hell, he thought, the brakes squealing as he made a U-turn and returned to his parents. Twenty minutes later, a good two dozen boxes marked "Christmas—outside" sat on the porch or in the yard, along with an untold number of heavy-duty extension cords and plugs-on-a-stick.

Take that, world, he thought as he dumped out enough icicle lights to doll up the Empire State Building.

"What on earth is the boy doing?"

Taking a moment to let the buzzing in her brain subside, Roxie broke her gaze from her phone to see Charley stand-ing at the brand-new, double-paned window. Around which hung motionless draperies, praise be. Eden, who'd arrived with her dog before Roxie was even up, was in the kitchen—which she'd declared "a miracle"—chopping vegetables

and whatnot for stew. And singing a tune from *Oklahoma!*
Things would most definitely never be the same.

In many ways.

As if in a dream, Roxie got up to peer out the window.
Across the street, Noah looked like a fly caught in a web of
icicle lights, desperately struggling to break free—a sight
that tickled her almost as much as it made her want to
weep.

"It would appear he's putting up Christmas decorations,"
she said. "Trying to, anyway."

"That's Gene's job…oh. Right." Charley paused. "I'm
gonna guess he has no clue what he's doing."

Roxie laughed, despite the weird, tight feeling in her
chest. "I think that's a safe bet," she said, heading to the
closet for her heaviest sweater-coat.

"Where you going?"

"To help. Wanna come?"

"Not on your life. Although I might dig out the Christmas wreath if the mood strikes." Her uncle settled into
his overstuffed chair, grabbing his glasses and half-read
mystery off the table beside it. Then he looked over the
glasses at Roxie. "You gonna tell him?"

"I don't know. Because it's not settled yet," she said to
Charley's raised brows.

"Sounded pretty settled to me, from what I just heard."

"Then not settled in my head. I need some time to get
used to the idea myself, before I go blabbing about it to all
and sundry."

"Noah's hardly all and sundry. And that didn't keep you
from telling anyone who'd stand still long enough about the
Atlanta thing—"

"I am capable of learning from my mistakes," Roxie said,
grabbing her mittens off the table by the front door and
heading out into the cold, crisp morning, where all those

mistakes she'd declared herself so capable of learning from taunted her mercilessly from the sidelines. Creeps.

Noah glanced over the minute the front door closed irrevocably behind her, and she wondered how it was possible to be this conflicted and still function.

"You look like you could use some extra hands," she called as she trooped down the steps.

He grinned the grin of the completely beleaguered, and her stomach went all disco fever on her. "Only if they're yours."

Now across the street, she forced herself to traverse his lawn, the dry, brown grass crunching underfoot as she came closer, telling herself turning tail right now would be totally lame. "How's your dad?"

"Doing pretty good, thanks. Should be home tomorrow, in fact. But…" Noah's gaze swept the house. "But ever since I can remember, the decorations went up without fail the day after Thanksgiving. And since Dad can't…" Noah cleared his throat, then looked at Roxie again, one side of his mouth lifted. "Do you remember what the yard looked like? When you were here in high school?"

"Like the mother ship had landed," she said, hating the gentleness in his voice, her susceptibility to it, as she bent over to open one of the boxes. "Wow. Inflatables?"

Noah chuckled. "We'd gone to Wal-Mart a few years back to get some replacement bulbs. I still remember the look on Dad's face when we walked through the door and spotted the display. Like a little kid, I swear. I also remember the look on *Mom's* face when we came home with not, one, not two, but *three* of the damn things. There's also a lit-up train that goes around the whole yard. On tracks."

"Ohmigosh," Roxie said on another laugh. "You're kidding? No wonder he starts so early—it must take a week to get it all done!"

"Something like that, yeah. Depending on how many of us he can strong-arm into helping him." He scanned the yard, as though envisioning the scene. "Dad gets a real kick out of watching the kids when they come to see it all," he said before his eyes touched hers again. "And I know he'd be disappointed if they showed up and there was nothing to see. Here. Take this end."

He handed Roxie the plug end of the lights, slowly walking backward, patiently untangling as he went, just as he patiently dealt with his father's foibles every day…and she understood. Why he was out here freezing his butt off, why he put up with Gene's nagging, all of it. Because for all their differences, their bond was indissoluble. Although to be honest, it almost made her mad, that someone so obviously devoted to his family couldn't see his way clear to start one of his own.

"This is definitely much easier with two people," Noah said, the recalcitrant lights yielding far more quickly with four hands prying them apart.

"Most things are," she said.

His eyes cut to hers, then away. "Dad put me in charge of the business."

"Really?" He nodded. "Temporarily, or…?"

"He said from now on, but who knows?" That strand set to rights, Noah carefully laid it on the porch and dumped the next one out of its box. "Except I can tell he had… reservations. That if he hadn't had that heart attack he never would have handed over the reins, unless…" He yanked too hard on the strand. "Unless I'd met his conditions."

"The same ones from before?"

"I imagine so. And you know what?" he said on a frosted breath. "It sucks that I'm nearly thirty and still feel like I have to fight for my father's approval. That no matter what,

I still come up short in his eyes. Why the hell should it even matter?"

Okay, so maybe not *that* patient. Not that she didn't understand that, too. The closer the relationship, the more tangled it was likely to be. Like the lights.

"It matters because you love him," she said gently, even as her stomach sank, remembering what Gene had asked of her the day before. "Everybody wants their parents to be proud of them." His only reply was a grunt. "What are you going to do?"

"Work my butt off. Make sure I don't give him any reason to regret his decision. And maybe…" His eyes swung to hers, and electricity shot through her.

"What?"

He gave her a long, hard look that sent another hundred megawatts or so crackling along her skin. But instead of finishing his thought, he handed her the strand of lights. "Hang on to this while I get the ladder?"

He'd barely gotten ten feet before she blurted out, "I got a job offer."

And when he whipped around, she saw in his eyes exactly what she'd suspected he'd stopped himself from saying.

Not funny, God, she thought. *Not funny at all.*

Chapter Ten

"Where?" Noah said, the only word he could squeeze past the knot in his throat.

"Austin."

"How…?"

"It was really weird, actually," Rox said, with a short, nervous laugh. "Out of the blue, my former college roommate—we lost track of each other years ago—friended me on Facebook. Turns out she's a designer now, in Austin. Which is her hometown. Anyway, long story short, we started texting, then she called me…and it turns out she also owns this funky little furniture and collectibles store, and she's looking for someone knowledgeable to take over the merchandising because she's about to have a baby. So when she found out I was looking for a job—"

"She said it was yours."

"On the spot. With the possibility of becoming a partner some day. I even get to go on shopping trips all over the world, can you imagine?"

Although she was obviously trying to soft-pedal the news, there was no keeping the excitement out of her voice. Or her eyes. "When did this happen?"

"Actually, we've been on the phone all morning, ironing out the particulars." Her nose was turning red; she scrounged a tissue out of her pocket and wiped it. "I said I needed to give Naomi two weeks' notice."

Noah slowly lowered himself onto the cold porch steps, reminding himself they'd firmly established they didn't want the same things, that a relationship between them would have never worked. Not to mention he'd known all along she wasn't going to stick around.

Reasonable arguments, every one. And yet…

After a long pause, Roxie came and sat beside him, linking her arm through his. "This wasn't supposed to happen," she whispered, leaning her head on his shoulder. Which, because logic was clearly not his friend right now, felt inexplicably right.

"This?"

"Us."

Noah covered her hand with his. Swallowed hard. "The funny thing is, before you announced you'd found that job, I'd almost said—"

"That we should give it a shot? See where it goes?"

"Yeah," he breathed out.

"To make your father happy?"

He craned his neck to look at her. "You actually think I'd hook up with somebody just to please Dad?" She shrugged against his arm. "Honey, he's been on my case about this for years. Believe me, if all I'd wanted to do was shut him up I could've gotten hitched long ago."

"Why is that not making me feel better?" she said, and he chuckled.

"Only telling it like it is. But…even as I considered

asking if you were game, I knew it wasn't fair to you. Or right." He rubbed her arm for a moment, gathering his thoughts. "The thing is…it really does feel different. With you, I mean. I actually *like* you. I like being *with* you, talking to you. And I don't doubt for a minute we'd have a lot of fun in bed. Still and all, whenever I think of the next step…I choke."

"It's okay—"

"Dammit, Rox—would you stop being so reasonable? It's not okay, it's messed up, is what it is."

"Except, it would have never worked anyway, right? I'm leaving in two weeks, you've g-got obligations here…" *Ah, hell,* he thought as she said, in a small, mad voice, "I *knew* it was stupid to let myself fall for you. Knew we'd never see eye-to-eye on certain major issues. And for damn sure I wasn't about to go through that again, not after Jeff. But it was like…knocking a glass off the counter, when you all you can do is stand there and watch it fall, knowing it's going to crash into a million pieces."

Tell me about it, Noah thought, his heart fisting in his chest. Then he slung his arm around her shoulder and pulled her to him again, rubbing his cheek in her hair. "I'm so sorry, honey."

"For what? Being who you are?" She paused, skimming one fingertip over a varnish stain on the knee of his jeans. "I was *so* sure, as long as I didn't sleep with you I'd stay in control." She made a *pfft* sound through her lips, then sighed. "But that's not *your* fault. I still could've been more careful with the glass, made sure not to leave it on the edge. And I didn't."

"Because you're still not over Mac?"

"No!" Roxie lifted her head to look at him, her gaze steady despite the crease between her brows. Then her mouth scrunched on one side. "Okay, to be honest, you do

remind me of him in some ways. Or did, before I got to
know you. But when I moved on from Jeff I apparently left
Mac behind as well." She nestled her head on his shoulder
again. "Believe me, buddy, whatever I feel for you, I feel for
you. Not as a memory or a placeholder, but as somebody I
think is amazing in his own right."

He snorted. "Amazing?"

Her soft laugh vibrated against his shoulder before she
looked at him again. "It's true. Screwed up though this may
be, at least I've got that part straight in my head. I'm not
confusing you with anybody else. Cross my heart."

That makes one of us, Noah thought with a twist to his
gut. "So…what do you want to do now?"

Roxie pushed herself to her feet, backing into the yard
to look up at the porch. "Finish decorating this house, for
starters."

"That's not what I'm talking about."

Her troubled gaze fell to his. "I suppose, by rights, we
should call it quits now."

Noah stood as well. "Because pretending each other
doesn't exist in a town the size of a peanut is going to work
so well?"

"I hate this," she muttered, and he pulled her into his
arms again.

"We could just play it by ear, you know," he said into
her hair.

"Except—"

"Clothes will stay on. Promise."

She leaned back, frowning. "You sure you're okay with
that?"

"Strangely enough, yeah." His heart hammering in his
chest as he thought, *Dude, who* are *you?* "Because, you know
that bonding thing? I'm thinking, in this case, you wouldn't
be the only one with a problem if we fooled around."

"He said, gritting his teeth—"

"I'm serious, Rox." His hands moved to her shoulders so he could look her in the eyes. "Unless one or the other of us changes our mind about what we want, long term. And somehow I'm not seeing that happen. So," he said, releasing her, "we better get our rears in gear if we have any hope of getting this done before Dad gets home tomorrow."

Then he turned to drag the first of many reindeers and bears and such out of their oft-taped boxes, silently chewing out fate's ass.

"What are they doing now?" Charley asked Eden, who, her stew on the stove, apparently had nothing better to do than stand at the window holding her little dog and watching the goings-on across the street. And report to Charley.

"Hard to tell from here—if I'd known, I would've brought my opera glasses—but after he hugged her, they talked some more and now they've gone back to decorating the house. No kissing, though. So kinda inconclusive."

Charley pushed himself out of the nice, comfy chair and joined her at the window, exchanging distrustful glances with the dog. "You think she told him?"

Eden turned her head, making the wide-neck black sweater she was wearing slide off one shoulder, exposing a bright red bra strap. "While I'm far from deaf," she said, tugging it back up, "I don't have supersonic hearing. Nor am I clairvoyant."

"Oh, I don't know about that," Charley said, thinking about that shoulder. And where it led. "You always seem to guess right when I'm about to...you know."

Eden rolled her eyes and looked back out the window, only to smile when Charley bumped his hip into hers, not even caring when the dog growled at him. "Looks like

they're gonna be a while," he said, giving her moony eyes.
"Wanna mess around?"

"Actually, I think we should follow their example and
do some decorating ourselves." She set down the dog, who
gave her a dirty look before mincing over to plop in her
leopard print bed by the fireplace. "Give the place some
holiday cheer."

"I'd much rather you give *me* some holiday cheer."

"You got your holiday cheer this morning, you can wait
a few hours for the next dose. So whatcha got? In the way
of decorations, I mean?"

Charley pushed out a loud, pity-me sigh and started for
the garage, marginally cheered when, chuckling, Eden
grabbed his hand and pulled him back around to give him
a compensatory kiss, and he suddenly felt so happy it nearly
made him dizzy.

Then he glanced out the window one last time at his
mixed-up niece, so determined to get what she wanted she
couldn't see it was smack dab in front of her face. "I know
it's not up to me to fix her, but it seems so...unfair."

"She's a smart girl. She'll figure it out," Eden said.

But the question was, he wondered as Donna's old Jeep
Cherokee pulled into the driveway, would Noah?

His mother got out of her beat-up Explorer, a big, goofy
smile stretching across her face as she took in what they
were doing. "I can't believe you even thought about this."

"Day after Thanksgiving means leftovers and decorating," Noah said. "Wouldn't seem right otherwise. Besides,
I thought it would cheer Dad up."

"Or tick him off that he didn't get to do it himself,"
Donna muttered, then sighed. "To be honest, I'd totally
forgotten until I overhead one of the nurses talking about

setting up her tree." Then she noticed Roxie. "And how on earth did *you* get dragged into this?"

"Believe it or not, I volunteered," she said, and his mother shot him a look that plainly said, *Good Lord, she's as crazy as we are*. "How's Gene doing?"

His mother did a *you don't want to know* hand waggle, then tromped around to the back of the car and opened the hatch, the sun flashing off the silver clasp thing holding up most of her hair. "He's coming home tomorrow. If they don't kick the big pain in the patoot out sooner." Except it was perfectly obvious how scared she'd been of losing that pain in the patoot. Peering into the car, she shook her head. "Since I was in Santa Fe, anyway, I figured I may as well pick up a few things at Sam's Club. Big mistake."

Aside from the normal supplies—toilet paper and paper towels and eighteen packs of tomato and chicken noodle soup—everything else was for his father. Plaid shirts and a new pair of slippers. Hardback novels by two of his favorite writers. A treadmill. And—

"You can't be serious?" Noah hauled the boxed inflat-able—an eight-foot-tall snow globe sheltering a trio of car-oling polar bears—out of the depths of the truck. Behind him, Roxie giggled. "And you can just hush," he said, and she giggled harder, which only made Noah more morose, thinking about how much he was going to miss making her laugh.

"So you're not the only one who wants to cheer him up," Mom said. "And anyway, when you love somebody you give them what makes them happy." She made a face at the inflatable's box. "Even when it hurts." Then she looked at Roxie and smiled, and Noah heard the Gong of Doom go off in his head. "Honey, why don't you come inside and help me make up a couple of turkey sandwiches?"

* * *

"I'll never understand," Donna said, shoving up her sweater sleeves as she regarded the inside of her refrigerator, "how I can feed so many people at Thanksgiving and still have this many leftovers. There's ham, too, if you like. And I suspect—" she hefted the turkey carcass to the counter "—you're well aware I don't need help to make a few sandwiches."

"Yeah," Roxie said, sitting at the kitchen table, "I kinda figured you had that down by now. So what's up?"

One eyebrow lifted. "Why don't you tell me?"

"Is this you being mama bear looking out for her cub?"

Donna laughed. "As if I could. And anyway, the cub is plenty able to look out for himself. Has been for some time. Which I've been told in no uncertain terms. However, after raising a whole slew of cubs, Mama Bear is extremely observant. And nosy." Peeling back the foil, she cut her eyes to Roxie. "I've never seen him act around any other gal the way he does around you. You ask me, he's got it bad."

Heat flooding her face, Roxie lowered her eyes, worrying a little silver ring on her pinkie her mother had given her when she turned sixteen. "I accepted a job in Austin. This morning. I start in a couple of weeks."

"Oooh." Donna's brow crinkled. "I see. Does Noah know?"

"Yeah. I just told him," she said, adding, because she'd only promised Gene she wouldn't say anything to *Noah,* "did his dad tell you why he wanted me to come to the hospital?"

"No, as a matter of fact." Donna hauled a carving knife out of a block in front of her and start shaving off slices of white meat, then glanced in Roxie's direction. "I'm not gonna like this, am I?"

"Probably not. He did everything but promise me a dowry if Noah and I got together."

"Oh, Lord, that man," Donna sighed out. The knife set down, she turned, her arms crossed under her breasts. "Although with you going to Austin, I suppose the point is moot, anyway."

"Heh," Roxie said, thinking, *So this is hell. Colder than I expected, but whatever.*

"Oh, honey…love really sucks sometimes, doesn't it?"

Figuring there was no point in denying it, Roxie got up and snatched a piece of cut turkey, cramming it into her mouth. It wasn't chocolate, but sometimes you can only work with what you're given. "I feel like I've been ambushed," she muttered, chewing.

"That's pretty much the way it goes," Donna said, handing her another piece of turkey.

"It's so unfair." With great difficulty, Roxie swallowed the dry turkey mush in her mouth. "Noah was supposed to be the same Good Time Joe he was in high school. In fact, you have no idea how much I counted on that. He wasn't supposed to have…grown up."

Donna smiled. "It does happen eventually. Even to boys."

"Except…he still doesn't see himself doing the kids-and-mortgage thing. Which doesn't make him less of a grown-up, but it does mean I could never do what Gene asked. Even if I wasn't leaving." She tried to swallow again, only to nearly choke. Donna yanked a bottle of organic milk from the fridge, pouring a glass and handing it to Roxie. She washed down the mashed turkey, then said, "Which should be a solution, right? Out of sight, out of mind? So why do I feel like I'm being ripped apart inside?"

On a soft moan, Noah's mother took Roxie into her arms, holding her tight for several seconds before releasing her to snitch her own piece of turkey. "You know...nothing ever scared that boy growing up. Nothing. And he's got the scars to prove it." She wagged the turkey at Roxie. "So why the idea of settling down, having kids of his own, rattles him so badly, I have no idea."

Sipping her milk, Roxie walked over to the window to watch Noah set up a family of lit reindeer on the front end of the lawn. "Me, either. But damn...it seems such a *waste*."

A soft chuckle preceded, "Do you trust the goofball?"

Roxie wheeled around. "You're calling your own son a goofball?"

"Oh, you have no idea some of the things I've called my boys over the years. Well?"

A second or two passed before Roxie slowly nodded. "Yes, I do. Because he's never played the player with me. He's always been totally up front about his expectations. We both have, actually."

"Then the foundation is there, believe it or not. Now all you can do is have faith that if this is meant to work out, nothing or no one can stop it."

Roxie smiled, not having it in her to disabuse the woman of her fantasies.

Noah walked into the office and shut the door, barely muffling the noise from a half dozen power tools doing their thing. The past few days had been beyond busy. Not that Noah couldn't handle it, he was handling it all just fine—and loving it—but between his dad's return home on Saturday and his consequently needing to help his mother out, then his diving headfirst into his new duties even before the shop reopened after the holidays, he hadn't seen Roxie since the day after Thanksgiving. Meaning he felt like a game show contestant playing against a relentlessly ticking clock.

"Lunch?" he said when she answered Naomi's phone.

"Oh, um…really swamped here," she said, her voice sounding strange. And strained.

"Dinner, then? Although it might be late, I'm not getting out of here before seven these days—"

"Can't. Charley and I are going to Eden's—"

"Boss?" Benito said as he opened the door, knocking as an afterthought. "Oh, sorry—didn't realize you were on the phone."

Waving Benito inside, he said, "Tomorrow?"

"I'll call you, how's that?" she said. And hung up.

Noah frowned at the phone for a couple of seconds before clipping it back on his belt. His father's—now his—right-hand man frowned in concern.

"Everything all right?"

"Not sure," Noah said, feeling like his brain was stuffed with Silly Putty. "You need me?"

"Yeah. Thought you'd want to look over these specs for that new job before we get started."

Forcing himself back to the present, Noah considered the barrel-chested, bulbous-nosed man in front of him, who'd been working for his father since before Noah was even born. Who'd taught him even more than his father had. And who probably needed him to sign off on a project about as much as he needed Noah to teach him Spanish.

"You really think that's necessary?"

Thick, salt-and-pepper brows lifted on a weathered face. "I jus' figured, you'd want to do things like your dad."

One side of Noah's mouth lifted. "Which doesn't answer my question."

He could see the older man try to hide his smile underneath his heavy mustache, but it wasn't working. "I like to think of myself as a smart man, Mr. Noah. Smart enough to play the game however the boss man wants. No skin off my nose, you know?"

Dude was a master of diplomacy, that was for sure. "And what if I said I completely trust you to handle things on your end? Probably a lot better than I would."

Benito gave him a quizzical look. "I'm real flattered. But in this case, your daddy had the right idea, making sure at least two people know what's going on. So if it's all the same to you, I'd feel better having that second set of eyes."

"Then I'm good with whatever works for you."

The foreman nodded, then said, "Anything else?"

"Yeah. That you won't laugh too hard at my stupid questions."

"Not sure I can promise that," Benito said, his dark eyes sparkling. "Damn, it seems like yesterday when you were a baby, coming in here with your daddy an' building towers outta wood scraps over there in the corner. And now, here you are. The boss."

"*You* think that feels weird?"

Benito chuckled, then clamped his meaty hand around Noah's upper arm. "You know something, it takes a real man to admit he doesn't know it all. You're gonna make Mr. Gene real proud of you."

"That's what I'm hoping," he said, as the nonconversation with Roxie replayed in his brain, and he realized he'd never be able to fully concentrate on business until he figured out what was going on with her. Getting up to snag his barn coat off the rack by the door, he nodded in the general direction of the desk. "I need to go out for a while. Can you hold down the fort?"

"Sure thing. No problem," Benito said with a wide smile. Then he winked. "Although it might cost you."

The coat half on, Noah frowned at the other man. "How much does—did—my father pay you?"

The other man snorted. "Not enough. Not that I'm not grateful for the work—"

"Say no more." Noah hiking the coat onto his shoulders, digging in the pocket for his keys. "I'm not that familiar with the finances yet, but let me talk it over with Silas, see what we can do."

Affection gleamed in the man's dark eyes. "You know, sometimes you hear about these family businesses, the father passes it along to his kid, and the kid doesn't want it, or isn't interested, or the whole thing goes to hell in a handbasket, you know?" He shook his head, then extended his hand. "I'm proud to work for your daddy for more than thirty years. And God willing, I'm proud to work for you for thirty more."

"Same goes, Benito," Noah said, clapping the man's hand and giving it a hearty shake before heading toward the door. "I won't be long."

"Take your time, boss," he heard behind him. "Everything's under control."

In there, *maybe,* Noah thought as he stomped out to his truck. In his head, *not so much.*

Chapter Eleven

Funny, Roxie thought—when she looked up from the clinic's computer to see Noah looming over her—how you think you've got your feelings about somebody all sorted out until there they are, in front of you, and suddenly you don't know squat. Especially when the sight of the looming somebody makes your mouth go dry and your stomach turn inside out, and pheromones are flitting about like frakking sugarplum fairies.

"Noah! What on earth are you doing here?"

Angling his head toward the doctor's open office door, he called out, "Hey, Naomi—you got a problem with me taking Rox out for lunch?"

"What? Now hold on just a minute—!"

"Not at all," the doctor said, coming to the door. At which point Roxie shot her a you're-not-helping glare. "Although Roxie might."

She turned the glare on Noah. "Thought I said we were busy?"

Noah glanced around the empty waiting room, prompting Naomi to say, "Yeah, I know. Slowest afternoon we've had in forever. Can't believe it myself."

"A lull," Roxie said. "It'll pick up. With appointments. And things."

"So where you taking her?" Naomi said.

"Evangelista's. Where else?"

"Oh! Bring me back a couple of cinnamon rolls, would you?" She dug in her pocket for a five-dollar bill, handed it to Noah. "And a cup of coffee?"

"Oh, see," Roxie said, banging her knee as she sprang up from behind the desk. "I need to make coffee, I can't go."

"Baby," Naomi said, "you know I adore you, but you can't make coffee to save your life."

Pocketing Naomi's five—because, you know, Roxie was just a bystander, this had nothing to do with her—Noah gave her a funny look. "You can't even make coffee? Now that's sad. Get your coat, it's freezing out there."

"I can't, I've got—" At Noah's glower, she muttered, "Fine," and trudged to the closet.

"What's this all about?" she said, once they were in Noah's truck. Black. Like a hearse. Fitting, somehow.

"You want to call it off, then call it off. Because this avoidance crap is not you."

Okay, that was her bad, hoping he'd be so busy this thing between them would simply die a natural death, and she wouldn't have to actually act on the conclusion she'd come to the moment she saw all that *hope* in his mother's eyes. "I don't want to have this discussion in the truck—"

"Or on the phone, or probably not at Ortega's, either.

Well, tough. We're together for the first time in days. We're talking."

"I thought men didn't like talking."

"Never said I liked it. But you do what you gotta do. Now." He pulled the truck into the restaurant's parking lot. "We can chat out here where it's freezing, or go inside where it's warm. And where there's food. I haven't had lunch and I'm starving."

Brother.

Roxie marched through the spicy-scented restaurant to a small table at the end of a wildly colorful, primitive landscape mural and plopped down, Noah following suit. Evangelista, the mostly Mexican restaurant's bosomy owner, took one look at the pair of them, dropped menus and waddled discreetly away. Roxie smacked hers open, even though she'd memorized the damn thing in high school, only to smack it closed again. Noah was staring a hole through her. Since this wasn't going away, she said, "Noah, look. I don't know what got into us the other day, what got into *me,* but—"

"But you changed your mind."

"I came to my senses!" Leaning forward, she lowered her voice, even though the only other patrons were four cowboys from some ranch or other, laughing it up in a booth on the other side of the room. "What's the point of torturing ourselves? I'm leaving, you're staying, we still don't want the same things."

"Yeah. Got that. But I thought we were at least friends—"

"You guys ready to order?" Evangelista said, setting a basket of chips and a small bowl of salsa between them.

"Three tamale plate," Noah said, handing her the laminated menu but not taking his eyes off Roxie. "Red on the side, corn, potatoes. Oh, and two cinnamon rolls and a large coffee to go."

"Got it. And you, doll-baby?"

"Fried ice cream."

Noah frowned at her. "For lunch?"

"I'll eat my veggies tonight. Promise. And that friendship thing," she said after Evangelista waddled away again, "doesn't work for me, okay? And don't you dare give me that look, we already established things between us had gotten a little…wonky." At his continued staring, she went on. Like a runaway train, gack. "See, you're a guy, you can separate your feelings into these nice, neat compartments—friendship here, sex there, love way the heck over there somewhere. In theory, anyway. But turns out I can't really do that. At least, not with you. And *damn* you," she said, her face reddening, "for being everything I've ever wanted and everything I can't have. I mean, have you *watched* yourself with kids? With Eli's newborn?" She grabbed a chip and dunked it in the salsa, muttering, "Jerk."

Dipping his own chip, Noah glanced at her. With, to his credit, a troubled look in his eyes. "You done?"

Exhausted, Roxie sagged back against the chair as Evangelista brought their food. Roxie grabbed her spoon and gouged out her first bite so fast the woman snatched back her hand. "I think so," she said around a mouthful of hot crunch and cold, smooth sweetness.

This time Noah waited until they were alone again before saying, "Okay, you wanna know the truth? The friendship thing doesn't work for me, either."

Bent over her dessert mountain, Rox lifted her eyes to his. "Meaning you *do* want sex?"

"Was that ever even a question? You make me so hot my core temperature goes up a good five degrees every time I look at you."

"Flatterer," she said around another blissfully anesthetizing mouthful.

"Which doesn't happen as often as you might think," he said, and she *hmmphed*. At which point he leaned across the table and grabbed her hand, and the look in his eyes wasn't doing a blessed thing to cool her off. "Or at least not as much. That's gotta count for something."

"Yes, Noah, we have great chemistry. Still not enough. Not for what I want. Dammit," she whispered. Wiping her mouth on her paper napkin, she stared at the decimated mound of Frosted Flake-coated ice cream, angry that her eyes were stinging. "What do *you* want?"

"From you?"

"From me, for yourself…whatever."

"I want…things to be different."

At the genuine misery in his eyes, Roxie sighed around the clenched fist in her own chest. "But they're not."

"And…maybe they could be."

"Maybe? Could? Do you even hear yourself?" Jabbing her spoon into the ice cream, she crossed her arms and leaned back in the chair, her forehead pinched so tightly it hurt. "So, what? I should blow off the best job offer I've ever had in my life on the off chance that *maybe* you'll change your mind? That *maybe* I won't get my heart broken again? Holy heck, Noah—nobody knows better than I do that there are no guarantees, but there is such a thing as minimizing the risks!"

She shook her head. "I don't want an affair, Noah. I'm simply not wired that way. I thought you understood that. I guess I was wrong. And you should eat, your food's getting cold."

"Not hungry," he mumbled, signaling to Evangelista to bring a take-out box. "Finished?"

Amazingly, she was. Although she wasn't entirely sure he was talking about her "meal." His food boxed, Noah paid at the register and picked up Naomi's bagged rolls and coffee, then walked ahead of her to his truck, yanking open the passenger side door but saying nothing, the suffocating silence cocooning them as they drove back to the clinic. Where Noah finally said, "Just so you know? I've never cared one way or the other before whether a gal stuck around or not."

"Never?" His gaze fixed out the windshield, he shook his head, and she sighed. "Still no cigar, sweet cheeks."

Tortured eyes glanced off hers, then away again. "I know."

She waited a moment, then said, very softly, "This is killing me, too, Noah. On the one hand, I already know how much it's going to hurt, leaving. On the other..." She waited until he faced her again. "I also know how much it would hurt if I stayed."

When he didn't say anything, she snatched Naomi's bag off the console, then grabbed the door handle, only to gasp when warm, strong fingers clamped around the back of her neck and brought their mouths together. And if it'd been anybody but Noah, she would've clobbered the bejeebers out of him. Instead of, you know, letting herself fall into the sweetest, hottest, deepest kiss of her life. When it was over—approximately a year later—she said, through a tear-clogged throat, "And *that's* why I'm glad I'm leaving."

When she went to open the door this time, he didn't stop her.

"...and that's about it," Roxie said to Thea Griego, the clinic's new receptionist. "Everything's pretty straightforward, actually. Although you can call me on my cell anytime if you have questions."

Seated behind the silver garland-festooned reception desk, the pretty blonde grinned up at her. Married to a handsome rancher and mama to a rambunctious toddler boy, Thea had brought little Jonny in for a check-up when she'd heard about the job opening. Gal had jumped at it like a cat on a fly.

"Heaven knows, this is a lot easier on the back and feet than waitressing," she said with a low laugh, referring to her pre-marriage, pre-mama life. "And now that Jonny's old enough to hang out more with daddy, I figured it was time for me to spread my wings. So this is gonna be perfect."

One more thing settled, Roxie thought a few minutes later as she drove back to Charley's through a powdery, Christmas card snow. Even though it was only the middle of the afternoon, it was so dark some people had turned on their Christmas lights, and all the twinkly cheeriness was making her a little melancholy.

Okay, a lot melancholy.

Despite her best intentions, she had to admit the sleepy little town had grown on her. There was a lot of good here. A lot of love. She suspected she was going to miss it a lot more than she would have believed a few months ago, when she'd felt like a failure, having to move back. And of course there was Noah, whom she hadn't seen since the fried ice cream episode a week ago. Not sure who was avoiding whom, but he hadn't even come to his parents' family night dinner last Thursday.

And yes, she knew that because she'd looked for his truck in front of the house. So sue her.

Speaking of his parents' house…it was blazing in full Christmas glory when she pulled into Charley's driveway alongside his much more modestly decorated abode. A single string of large colored bulbs hailing from before the Moon Walk stretched along the top of the porch, a battered wreath on the door. That was it. Not even Eden had been able to convince him how sorry it looked. And Lord knows she'd tried, Roxie thought with a smile as she let herself inside to be greeted by a gleeful black-and-brown fluff ball named, of all things, Stanley.

"And you can take that mutt right back to the pound," Charley said before she'd even removed her coat, only to scoop the wriggling puppy into his arms and let him lick his chin.

"What'd he do now?"

"Only chewed up the new paperback I just bought."

"All the more reason to get an e-reader."

Charley rolled his eyes. They'd had this discussion before. "So he can chew that up instead of a seven-buck paperback? I think not. What's that?" he said, looking at the check she'd dug out of her purse and handed to him.

"From the eBay sales."

Holding the check out where the curious pup couldn't get it, Charley let out a low whistle. "Holy crap."

"Yeah. You did really well."

His eyes swung to hers. "No, *you* did really well. Okay, okay, you can get down," he said to the now yipping dog, who, once on the floor, tripped over himself in his haste to scramble up onto the chair in front of the window and bark at the blinking lights across the street. Charley laughed, then turned back to Roxie. "Did you take a good commission for yourself?"

"You bet."

"Seriously?"

"No. Hey, if it hadn't been for you I'd've been homeless. This was the least I could do."

Eyes watering, her uncle pulled her into a hug. "I'm gonna miss you, you big pain in the butt."

"Same goes," she said, chuckling.

Then he let her go. "Just so you know…Edie's moving in after you leave."

"As in, she's giving up her apartment?"

"Doesn't make sense to keep two places. And this way she'll finally have a room for her crafts. And yes, I know it seems fast, but—"

"Charley," Roxie said, taking hold of his arms, "you are not obligated to explain anything to me. Your life, your heart, your house. Your happiness. Go for it."

"You really mean that?"

"I really do. Besides," she said, her gaze dropping to Stanley, gnawing on something he probably wasn't supposed to have, "Diva needs to be taken down a notch or two." Then she looked at her uncle again. "Being alone— when you don't want to be—sucks." She glanced over at the fragrant Noble fir taking up a quarter of the living room, looking more like a Mardi Gras float than a Christmas tree. "Especially at Christmas."

"You'll be back for the holidays, right?"

She shook her head. "I'm going to be way busy. But it's okay, I'll be with Elise and her husband, so I won't be alone," she said, not stopping in time the memories of Christmases as a kid with her parents...the fantasy Christmases she'd always imagined she'd be having by now, with a husband and children. *Cut it out, bitterness gives you wrinkles,* she thought, grateful when Charley practically lunged at the landline when it rang.

For a moment, Roxie considered telling her uncle about losing the baby, only to decide he really didn't need to know, that it would only make things more complicated. He'd worry, is what he'd do. Or go after Jeff with a pitchfork. And heaven knew, neither of them needed that.

Leave the past in the past, cupcake, she thought, looking outside at the gentle snow, like glittering pearls in the December dusk. Perfect for taking Stanley for a walk, to hopefully exorcise both the ickies from her brain and at least some of Stanley's puppy crazies. Not that she held out much hope for either, but it might be the last time she got to walk in the snow for a while, Austin not being generally known for its winter activities.

Bundled back up, the dog turning himself inside out trying to chew his new leash, she called to Charley—who'd disappeared upstairs—"Taking the dog for a walk!" and let them both outside, where the crisp, cold air soothed her frazzled nerves. And the deep hush as they shuffled through the confectioner-sugar snow—well, she shuffled, Stanley bounced—seemed to penetrate her very being.

Now that Thea had taken the helm at the clinic, there really was no reason for her to stick around. All the eBay auctions were done and the pieces shipped, the rest of Mae's things sorted and in storage for the estate sale she'd hold in six months or so. And Charley was on the brink of starting his new life with Eden, which Roxie gratefully realized she was more happy about than not.

"Guess it's time, Stanley," she said to the dog.

Then she shrieked when Noah said, "Time for what?" right behind her.

He hadn't meant to stalk her. Exactly. But when he walked out of his parents' house and saw her and the puppy starting down the street, something—sheer idiocy, most likely—pushed him after her.

"Where on earth did you come from?" she said, blinking at him as if he'd materialized out of thin air.

"Stopped by my folks' to give Dad an update. Saw you when I came out. Guess you didn't notice me in the snow."

"Um, no." She glanced away, then back. "How's your dad doing?"

"Excellent, actually. If the docs say it's okay, he and

Mom are going on a cruise, right after Christmas. To the Caribbean."

"Aw...that'll be nice."

The snow gently pinging their faces, they stood there like a couple of doofuses, Roxie apparently not knowing what to say any more than Noah. To break the awkwardness, if that was even possible, he squatted in front of the puppy, who bounded over to Noah like he'd been waiting to meet him his whole life. "Who's this?"

"Stanley. I got him for Charley. From the pound."

"Hey, guy," Noah said, laughing when the thing tried to heave himself into Noah's lap. "What is he?"

"Dog. Like one of those little sponge critters you put water on, you don't know what you've got until it's done growing."

The puppy having abandoned him to bark at the snow, Noah stood, chuckling despite the sting of seeing her again. His own damn fault, to be sure, nobody'd told him to follow her, to stir up again all those feelings he'd tried so hard to bury in work. "He'll be a good friend to Charley."

"Although he'll have to share him with Eden. She's moving in. As soon as I'm gone, apparently."

"With the rat dog?"

Roxie laughed. "I know," she said, watching Stanley chase his own tail, then fall over in the snow. "Should be interesting."

"You are so evil."

"I do what I can," she said, grinning up at him. "Anyway, Charley and Eden seem happy enough. But...would you and your folks mind keeping an eye out? Make sure he's okay?"

"You don't even have to ask, you know that."

She nodded, then they spoke together:

"So when are you going—?"

"I'm leaving tomorrow—"

Noah lost his breath. "Tomorrow? That soon?"

"Yeah, we found my replacement at the clinic. Everything's done here…there's no real reason for me to stick around." The dog yanked on the leash, nearly knocking her off balance. "Toss my clothes into a few suitcases and… head out. Rest of my stuff's in storage, I'll get it after I find my own place."

"Bet you can't wait," Noah said. Grumpily.

He thought maybe her eyes watered. "That's why I'm not," she whispered, then leaned forward, standing up on tiptoe to kiss his cheek. As she lowered herself he grabbed her hand.

"I really do wish you the best," he pushed past the pain in his chest. "Because nobody deserves getting what she wants more than you."

A tiny smile touched her lips. "Thank you," she said, then tugged the puppy to continue their journey. A journey on which Noah was clearly not invited.

And he had nobody but himself to blame for that.

Chapter Twelve

Elise Sugihara-Dickson looked, dressed and sounded exactly the same as she had in college, even if her shorter hair and all-black wardrobe—velvet leggings, flats with rhinestone-studded toes and a cowl-neck sweater the size of a circus tent to cover her enormous baby bump—were definitely much spiffier than the grungy Salvation Army getups the gal used to sport back in the day.

And the store—Oh. My. God. Cozily snuggled between a trendy, upscale clothing boutique and an equally trendy Asian fusion restaurant in downtown Austin, Fly Away Home was the stuff dreams were made of. At least Roxie's dreams, she thought as she tried to take it all in at once. Lord, she'd never seen so many pretties congregated in one two-story space in her life.

"Would it sound hugely unsophisticated of me to say, 'Wow'?"

Although the store was closed on Sundays, Elise had

brought Roxie to see the place without the distraction of customers and her other employees. Now she grinned. "Hell, I say pretty much the same thing every morning when I walk in," she said in her rapid-fire Southern accent. "Fun, huh?"

"Fun? It's practically a theme park."

"I know, right?" her old friend said, and they both laughed. From the moment they'd reconnected, it was as if no time had passed at all, their easy friendship picking up exactly where they'd left off. It had been nearly three in the morning before they got to bed, after Elise's husband, Patrick, finally lumbered out of their bedroom and pointed out the time. Roxie had forgotten how good it felt to have another gal to talk to.

"So you built this up all on your own?"

"Oh, Lord, no. Although the inventory's turned over several times since I bought the place about five, six years ago, from this dude who'd decided to retire. He had some neat stuff even then, and the location is *fabulous*. So when he offered me a deal I couldn't turn down, I jumped on it. 'Course, I'll be paying him off until I'm dead," she said with a shrug, "but it's totally worth it."

Her eyes as big as a kid's in a candy store, Roxie moved through a dozen vignettes, each one done in a different period, from early nineteenth century to art nouveau to midcentury modern to contemporary. "Where do you find all this stuff?"

"Estate sales, buying trips overseas. Wherever. You like it?"

"Are you kidding? I love it. All of it." She picked up a gorgeous art deco painted glass vase. "Especially since this is so not our mothers' antique store."

"You got it. Nice to know our tastes still mesh as well

as they did when we were sharing that dinky house near campus."

Roxie howled. "Ohmigosh, now I'm gonna have nightmares for a week. God, that place was ugly."

"Hey. At the time we thought we were seriously stylin'. That lime-green bathroom *rocked,* baby."

"Because it went so well with the burnt-orange shag carpet in the rest of the house."

"No, it *distracted* from the orange shag. As did the purple walls."

Roxie held up one finger. "Not purple. *Grape Mist.*"

"Thank God there's no evidence. If there'd been Facebook then, my career would be screwed—"

Elise's cell rang. She pulled it out of a hidden pocket in her sweater tent, chuckling when she checked the number. "The hubster. Suffers from heavy-duty pregnancy guilt, poor baby. Checks in at least once an hour to see how I'm doing. This won't take long. Go ahead and keep looking around."

The sting came out of nowhere. Honestly. Here she was, dream job landed, reconnected with a great friend…and about to tip over the edge from somebody else's domestic bliss? So lame.

Wasn't as if you left anything behind in Tierra Rosa, right?

If you didn't count her heart, not a thing.

She'd get over it, of course. Over Noah. Pining for what wasn't rightfully hers—and never had been—wasn't her style. God knew she was nothing if not a survivor, that for all its wounds, her heart kept on beating…and would find its way back to her, as it always had before.

Her life as a Celine Dion song. Yay, a new low.

"Rox? Hey. What's up?"

She spun around to find Elise frowning at her with don't-mess-with-me eyes. Too bad. "I think last night just caught up with me."

"Tell me about it," her friend said, yawning, then waved her toward the door. "Definitely seeing naps in both of our near futures. Oh, by the way…" She let Rox out first, then set the alarm before following. "Wanna check out a couple of local estate sales this weekend?"

Roxie glanced back, her thumb jerked over her shoulder. "Because it's not crammed to the rafters already in there?"

"Believe it or not, it doesn't stick around. If a piece doesn't find a home with a client or sell off the floor within three months, I eBay it. So there's always room for more! So, you up for some shopping?"

"Bring it on," Rox said, embracing the thrill of the hunt. That old optimism that everything she wanted was simply waiting for her to find it. And while she was at it? Maybe she could find a spare heart for cheap.

'Cause she needed to plug up this hole in her chest, fast.

For as long as Noah could remember Christmas mornings at his parents' house had been crazy. Factor in six grandkids under the age of seven, and it was flat-out insane. In the best definition of the word.

And normally Noah was right on the floor with them, tossing wadded up wrapping paper at his brothers and making Blue bark and his mom go, "Noah, for pity's sake!" at least every thirty seconds. This Christmas, however, even though he was still on the floor, still laughing when the kids crawled all over him, still genuinely touched by his mother's uncanny ability to give them all exactly the right gifts whether they'd dropped hints or not…he simply wasn't feeling the joy.

Nor was he doing a particularly good job of hiding it, if the not-so-subtle exchanged glances between assorted adult members of the family was any indication.

At long last the Great Christmas Carnage was over, the kids had all claimed assorted corners of the family room to play with their new toys, and all the females except Tess, who was feeding the baby, had swarmed into the kitchen where his mother was hollering out who wanted bacon and who wanted sausage, and did everybody want French toast or pancakes, she could do either, it wasn't any bother.

Exactly like every Christmas since he could remember.

Only this year, Noah felt as if somebody'd ripped a hole in his heart the size of the Grand Canyon. How the morning could make him miss Roxie so much, when she'd never been a part of his family's Christmases, he had no idea. But for damn sure, he wasn't "getting over" her. If anything, every day the painful irony only got worse.

Silas plopped beside him on the beat-up sectional, lightly slapping Noah's knee before crossing his arms high on his chest, his brows dipped behind his glasses. Groaning, Noah let his head drop back on the cushions.

"Let me guess—you drew the short straw."

"Oh, they didn't even bother with straws, just pointed and said, 'You're the oldest, you go talk to him.'"

"Nothing to talk about."

"Bull. You look like a dog left behind at the pound. Come on." Silas slapped Noah's knee again as he got up. "Get your coat, we're going outside."

"And if I don't want to?"

"It's me or Mom. Choose wisely, grasshopper."

Pushing out a heavy breath, Noah heaved himself out of the nice, soft cushions, grabbed his coat off the arm of the sofa and followed his brother outside into the frigid, blue-skied morning, the sun glinting off patches of frozen snow.

"Here's a news flash, bro," Silas said before they got to the end of the walk. "It's not a crime to be in love."

Nothing like coming straight to the point. "What makes you think—?"

"You're not seriously gonna argue?"

Noah was quiet for a long moment, then said, "I honest-to-God never thought it would happen. Not to me."

"So I gathered."

Jiggling his keys in his coat pocket, Noah frowned at his brother. "Except…if this is love, how come it hurts so much?"

Silas quietly chuckled. "You remember how we used to wrestle? When we were kids?"

"Like I could forget. I've *still* got bruises."

"As does Mom, I'm sure. But do you also remember that the more you struggled after you got pinned, the more it hurt?"

"And that if I didn't I'd get creamed. Or suffocate."

"Okay, so maybe not the best analogy. Still. Love's a lot like that. Once you stop resisting, it stops hurting. So." Silas crossed his arms. "You got any idea why you're fighting so hard?"

Another several seconds passed before Noah released another, softer, "I think so, yeah."

"Care to share?"

Noah's gaze landed on Charley's house across the street, a house without Roxie, as he wrestled with himself, about whether or not to give voice to the phantom thoughts he'd kept locked up in the back of his brain for so long he'd almost stopped hearing them. Until some curly-headed gal unwittingly unlocked their cage and set them free to run amok, screaming like freaking banshees in his ear.

"What difference does it make?" he said, his voice as harsh as the wind whipping down their ice-covered street. "I'm here. She's not. I can't leave, and I sure can't ask her to come back. Especially since…"

"Go on."

Noah looked away, his breath frosting around his mouth. "Since I seriously doubt I could ever live up to the example our folks set."

Silas gawked at him. "You're kidding me, right?"

"Nope."

"Wow. Nothing like being a little hard on yourself."

"It's called being realistic. And honest. And Roxie… no way would she ever settle for something half-assed. Or should she."

Silas flipped up his jacket collar against the back of his neck, the wind ruffling his hair. "So…the feelings are mutual?"

"Yeah," Noah said, already irritated for having said as much as he had. Although the release felt good, too. Then he laughed. "All the boneheaded things I used to do without even batting an eye? This makes me feel like I'm gonna hurl. That I don't know *how* to love somebody, that I'd screw it up, that I've *already* screwed up. That…" He pushed a swallow past his constricted throat, the wind making his eyes sting. "That I've lost her."

His gaze swung to Silas, who was angled away from him with his hands shoved in his pockets and his head bent, his mouth set. His brother's "thinking hard" pose, he knew. "Before," Noah went on, his heart knocking against his ribs, "either I knew I'd succeed or it didn't matter. But this…" The frigid air scraped his lungs when he hauled in a breath. "I don't have an idea in hell whether I'd be any good at this or not. And failure's not an option."

Several beats passed before Silas released a breath, then

looked at Noah again, his expression more relaxed. "For what it's worth, we've all been there. Nothing scarier than putting your heart out there."

"But you got married anyway. All of you. Even Jesse, and he was only *eighteen,* for God's sake."

"Don't discount ignorance," Silas said on a short, dry laugh. "It definitely has its uses." He glanced out at the street again. "What about kids?"

Yeah. That. Noah gave his head a sharp shake. "How one woman could turn everything I believed about myself on its head…I don't get it."

"Nobody does," Silas said, sympathetically clamping a hand on his shoulder. "Not that everyone who falls in love automatically thinks 'I wanna make babies with this person,' but it happens often enough to keep the species going." He let go to lean against the chunky stone pillar housing an old gas lantern that hadn't worked in years. "All of us go into this commitment thing blind," he said, "even when we think we've got a clue. And Mom and Dad would be the first ones to say that."

Noah frowned. "But…after Amy…?"

"How did I find the courage to try again?" He shrugged. "I don't think it's so much about finding it, as it is not ducking fast enough before it clobbers you over the head. It's just this voice that says…this is right. Along with, I suppose, a determination to *keep* it right. Of course, both people have to be on the same page about that," he said with a slight grimace, referring—Noah assumed—to his first wife's definite lack in that department.

"Dad! Uncle Noah!" Sunlight glanced off Ollie's straight blond hair when he opened the front door. "Gramma says to tell you breakfast's ready!"

"Coming, squirt," Silas said, then looked back at Noah. "So what are you going to do?"

"Hang myself?" Noah said, plowing his fingers through his hair. "It's not like I can simply up and leave, is it? All those years I've busted my buns to prove to Dad he can count on me...what *can* I do? Tell him, after less than a month, I've changed my mind? That some *girl* is more important than the business he spent his entire adult life building?"

"Is that all Roxie is? Some girl?"

His face heating, Noah looked away. "If she was, we wouldn't be having this conversation." Air left his lungs in a huge rush. "Man, am I between a rock and a hard place, or what?"

"Sure looks like it," Silas said, not being helpful at all. "But on the upside, at least now we all know you're human."

"Butthead," Noah muttered at his brother's grin, hugely tempted to cram a fistful of snow down his collar.

"You sure you don't want me to help?" Roxie asked Elise's husband, Patrick, as he carted off what was left of the ham to the kitchen. Both sets of Elise's and Patrick's boisterous, energetic parents had already gone, leaving behind a startled calm and a boatload of dirty dishes.

The gangly, graying blonde plunked the platter on the counter dividing the living area from the kitchen in their fabulous, eclectically furnished condo overlooking the Colorado River. "Nope. Got it covered."

"But you did all the cooking, you should let me do *something*."

"What you can do," Patrick said with a wide, slightly gap-toothed smile, "is keep Her Royal Highness from waddling in here and telling me I'm not loading the dishwasher right."

"It's true," Elise said with a shrug from her perch on

the tangerine-colored sofa, her puffy, fuzzy-socked feet stretched out in front of her. "I would. Because he tosses the dishes in there any old way, no respect for order at all."

Laughing, Roxie sank into the other end of the sofa, soaking in the soft glow of the colored lights on the retro silver aluminum Christmas tree and trying desperately to hang onto something that almost passed for contentment. It had been a lovely, lazy day, filled with laughter and friends and ending in the most amazing meal she'd ever eaten in her life. She absolutely loved her job. And in a week she'd be moving into her new apartment, an adorable one-bedroom in a quirky old Queen Anne not far from work.

Only then she'd have to return to Tierra Rosa to get her stuff out of storage, a thought which made the content-ment go *poof.* So to distract herself she focused on Pat-rick's bustling about the kitchen, humming to himself as he worked.

Big mistake.

"You've got a real keeper there," she said, not even trying to keep the wistfulness out of her voice.

Elise tried to shift, winced, then sighed a happy sigh. "And don't I know it. Although I had to kiss a hella lot of frogs before I found him. Astounding, the number of losers out there…oh. Sorry," she said, grimacing as she apparently remembered Jeff. "Can I blame it on the pregnancy?"

"Sure. And it's okay. I'm more than over *him,* believe me."

Oops.

Elise nudged Roxie's thigh with her foot. "And who is it you're *not* over?"

"I have no idea what—"

"Hey." Spearing Roxie with her dark, way-too-astute gaze, Elise said, "I'm sending you to Italy next month, last thing I need is you ending up in Bulgaria by mistake because some dude keeps pulling you to La La Land. So what's going on?"

It'd been years since she'd thought of how her mother could immediately tell when something was amiss, how a simple, "What's wrong?" could reduce Roxie to tears. Fighting the suckers now, she said, "Other than managing to once again fall in love with the absolutely worst possible person for me? Not a thing."

"You really need to stop doing that," Elise said, and Roxie sputtered a laugh. "So how did this one rate on the ol' Jerk-o-meter? Assuming Jeffrey was, what? A ten?"

"Ten, hell. Try twelve. And to be honest, I'd assumed Noah was at least a seven, maybe even an eight."

Elise handed her a box of tissues off the end table. "But…?"

"But it turns out he's actually…pretty darn close to perfect. Except for one or two tiny things."

"Oh, hell…he's gay."

Roxie laughed again, even as she dabbed at her leaking eyes. "Um, no. But he is allergic to white picket fences."

"Oh, sweetie…" Elise held out her hand, wagging for Roxie to take it. "I'm so sorry," she said with a gentle squeeze. "I'd give you a hug, but bending forward ain't happening these days." Then she whispered, "Was the sex good, at least?"

"We never got that far."

"You *sure* he's not gay?"

"My decision, not his. Because I knew…" She swiped at a hot tear trickling down her cheek. "Well. It seemed like a good idea at the t-time."

With great effort, Elise slowly swung her feet off the couch to sit up, gesturing for Roxie to scoot over so she could give her that hug, at which point Patrick—who'd known Roxie for all of two weeks and had clearly heard the entire conversation—mumbled something about men being dumb as bricks, which only opened the floodgates.

Because when it came to *dumb,* Roxie had 'em all beat, hands down.

"Do you believe this snow?" Noah's father said, stomping the damn stuff off his feet as he came inside the shop, his grin broad in a face still tan from the cruise.

Plans for a new project spread out on a drafting table right inside the door, Noah grunted. Normally he greeted the first snowfall of the season like an excited little kid, champing at the bit for snowball fights and sledding parties, rubbing his hands in glee at the prospect of navigating his truck through snow-choked, winding mountain roads. But this January—the snowiest on record, for which the New Mexico ski industry was extremely grateful—it only made him grumpy as hell.

"Everything okay?" Gene asked, stuffing his gloves inside his coat pocket.

Noah pushed his mouth into a smile. "Yeah. Fine."

At least on this front it was. Apparently, Gene's forced vacation had made him look at things from a whole new angle. Including, as it happened, Noah. Not a day passed that his father didn't tell him how well he was doing, how pleased he was. In fact, whenever Noah tried to defer to his dad when the old man was around, Gene backed off, saying, "Whatever you think is best, I trust you."

Who'dathunkit?

So now he waved his father toward the back of the shop. "Go take a look at the order Benito and them are working on, it's turning out fantastic."

But as his father trundled off—whistling, for God's sake—Noah's smile quickly crumpled into a glower. Because nothing felt right anymore. Felt like home. Ever since

Christmas, when he'd admitted out loud how bad he had it for Roxie, his skull had felt like a pressure cooker about to explode. And with every day that passed the discontent only grew deeper, choking out even the supreme satisfaction of proving to his father—and, okay, himself—that he was damn good at what he did. That, by making sure he had the best crew ever working with him, he could even juggle both the cabinetry and construction arms of the business.

And not drop a single ball.

By rights he should have been on top of the world. Victorious and vindicated. Instead, he simply felt...empty. Empty and alone and frustrated beyond belief.

The plans a blur, Noah threw down the pencil he'd been using to make notes and roared into the office to get his coat, still wrestling into it as he walked to his truck through a gentle blizzard of lazily floating flakes, as if somebody'd busted open a featherbed. The snow was too wet to stick to the roads, although the minute the sun went down that'd change. Now, however, it was safe enough to take a drive, clear his head. Although what he really wanted to do was bang that head against the steering wheel, maybe jar something loose. Or give himself amnesia so he'd forget about Roxie once and for all.

He drove away from town on a sparsely populated stretch of road that led past Garcia's Market, the Baptist church, a small storage facility...nearly running the truck off the road when he caught a glimpse of Roxie carting a big box around to the back of a U-Haul, the snow nearly turning her curls white.

Feeling as if King Kong was squeezing the hell out of his chest—and having no earthly idea what he was going to say—he drove up alongside the van and got out.

From the *Oh, crap* look on her face as he approached, it was pretty obvious she'd hoped they wouldn't run into each other. And if her heart was beating as hard as his was right now, her chest probably hurt like hell, too.

"Why didn't I know your stuff was stored here?"

Typically, though, she met his gaze dead on. "It never came up?"

"You could've asked me, I would've gladly brought it to you. Saved you a trip." *So take that,* he thought, as her brows lifted.

"Really?"

"Yeah. Really."

"Everything okay, Roxie?" her uncle called from a few feet away, shuffling through the snow, carrying a box.

"Yes, of course," she said with a glance in Charley's direction, then back at Noah, who could barely breathe for wanting to haul her into his arms. Get *over* the woman? In what universe?

Even through the snow he saw her cheeks redden before she cleared her throat. Behind her the van's loading door rumbled shut.

Noah slugged his hands into his coat pockets. "You sticking around for a bit?"

"No," she said on a pushed breath. "In fact, if you hadn't come along when you had, you would've missed me altogether. Hey, I hear you're doing great. With the shop and everything."

Fine. If that's the way she wanted to play, so be it. "I am." He paused. "How's the new job?"

"Everything I hoped it would be," she said, and he could tell by the way her eyes softened, she meant it. "And more. I was in Italy for a week. Going to France in the spring."

Want company? he almost said, suddenly imagining waking up in Paris with her snuggled up against him, naked and warm and smelling of faded perfume. And sex. Not that he'd ever been to Paris, but he could fill in the blanks as well as the next person. "Sounds great," he said flatly. "You seeing anybody?"

The question apparently caught her so off guard she reeled. "Um…no. Way too busy, for one thing."

His eyes trapped hers. "And for another?"

He watched probably a dozen possible responses flash behind her eyes before she finally said, "Not really interested, to tell the truth."

Noah felt the corner of his mouth tuck up. "You're not just saying that?"

Tears bulging over her lower lashes, she shook her head, and now King Kong planted his hairy butt right on Noah's chest. "No," she whispered, then swiped her mittened hand underneath her eyes, leaving snow stuck to her lashes. "How about you?"

Against his better judgment, Noah lifted a hand to brush away the tiny white clump. "You kidding?" he said softly, then turned and walked back to his truck. Yeah, just like that, like the whole thing had been a dream.

Or a nightmare.

Except, the minute he walked back inside the shop it was as if something really big and *really* loud bellowed *What the* hell *do you think you're doing?*

He stopped, looking around the shop, at what, up to that moment, he'd considered his life. The only thing he'd ever believed would be a constant in it. A second later his gaze landed on his father, joking with Benito as he showed a new hire the ropes, and he knew what he had to do. No matter how much it scared him.

Because, quite simply, if he didn't he'd die.

"Dad?" he called across the shop, waiting until his father's eyes met his before he said, "we need to talk."

God knew how long the banging on her front door had gone on before Roxie roused herself enough from her coma to hear it. Opening one eye, she saw it was barely eight, an unholy hour when you'd stayed up until nearly five unpacking.

She briefly considered ignoring the increasingly insistent knocking, only to decide it might be her landlady bringing her coffee cake or something equally yummy—which Mrs. Harris was prone to do, bless her seventy-something heart—and it would be rude to turn her away.

Yelling, "Just a sec!" Roxie heaved herself upright, shuddered at her Brillo-headed reflection in the mirror over the dresser, and grabbed her ratty chenille robe, yawning as she tied it closed on her way to the door. Through, she noted with disgust, stacks of boxes that had clearly multiplied during the night.

She briefly considered at least running a comb through her hair, decided Mrs. Harris wouldn't care—or see, being blind as a bat—before she yanked open the door.

And then shrieked.

Grinning around a lollypop stick, a beard-shadowed Noah straightened up from leaning against the doorjamb. "About damn time you answered the door." He pulled two Tootsie Roll pops out of his jacket pocket. "Cherry or chocolate?"

She had nothing. Speech, thought…all gone. Until, after roughly fifty years, "What…? How…?" finally screeched out, followed immediately by her realizing she looked like a haunted house reject and probably had morning breath and ohmy*god*, what was he *doing* here?

He waggled the Tootsie Roll pops. "Breakfast of champions," he said, and she took the cherry one, which she shakily unwrapped and stuck in her mouth, sucking on it like mad for several seconds before the sugar kick-started her brain enough to realize the man didn't come all the way here just to give her candy, and with a little cry, she threw herself across the threshold—nearly tripping over the doorjamb, natch—and into his arms, and then it was all about tangled tongues and knocking teeth and mixing cherry and grape and salty tears, and she grabbed his hand and yanked him inside, through the boxes and down the hall to her tornado-struck bedroom, where she proceeded to rip off his clothes, explanations could wait, she couldn't.

Apparently neither could he, praise be, and seconds later they were naked and joined, and she cried with the sheer bliss of his filling her, then cried again when he pushed her over the edge into a soaring free fall the likes of which they'd never believe down on the farm.

And when it was over, Noah gathered her close, both of them panting and sweaty, and said, "And here I was just hoping to score coffee," and she laughed so hard she started to sob, and he held her tight until she could breathe again. Could think.

Gently brushing her hair away from her temple, over and over, he whispered, "What was all that about being afraid to bond?"

"It was worth the risk," she said, then bit her lip.

And then he said, very gently, "God, I love you, Rox," and she burst into tears all over again. Jeebus.

Finally, she got out, "You're not just blowing air up my skirt?"

"That would be hard to do, seeing as you're not wearing one." And then she was laughing and crying at the same time. In his arms. Reasonably sure he was never going to let her go.

Even so…"Why?"

"Why what?"

"*Why* do you love me? If you even know, I mean—"

"Because you surprise me," he said easily. "And make me laugh. And when you smile it's like all the bad stuff in the world simply…goes away. And…" He paused, then lifted her chin to look into her eyes. "And you made me dig deeper inside myself than I ever have before. Which was scary as hell, because, man, it was like my folks' garage in there. But it's okay," he said over her chuckle, "because I know you'll never let the crap pile back up, ever again. That answer your question?"

"Very nicely, thank you," Rox said, feeling all warm and fuzzy as she laid her head back on his chest. Only to suck in an *oh, hell* breath. "Um…speaking of risks…we weren't using anything."

A long, long moment passed before Noah said, "And what's the worst that can happen? We make a baby?"

Feeling as though her curls had grown into her brain, Roxie struggled up enough to lean on Noah's chest and look down into his face. "You're not serious."

"After facing my father? And your uncle? And driving twelve straight hours to get here? Trust me, I'm serious. And if little whosits comes out with these," he said, fluffing her curls, "all the better." He kissed her, then said, "Marry me."

She stiffened. As, she noted, did he. Again. Wow. "What?"

"I can't live without you, Rox. Okay, I suppose I could, but I'd be miserable. Discovered I'm not real partial to being miserable. Or lonely. You messed with my head, lady," he said softly. Sweetly. Smiling. "Only one way to straighten it out. *Marry me.*"

Tears crowded her eyes. "I can't go back, Noah—"

"Not asking you to. I'll find work here. Or anywhere you go. Because I'm awesome," he said, and she laughed.

"But…your father," she said, sobering. "The business…?"

He tucked her head under his chin. "When I went to see

your uncle to get your address—and asked for his blessing, because it seemed like the thing to do—"

"You're kidding?"

"Nope. Think he got a big kick out of it, too. *Anyway,* when I made some noise about not being sure how this was all gonna work out, he quoted some Scottish dude who'd gone on an expedition to the Himalayas in the thirties. Something about…that without commitment, there's always this temptation to turn back. To give up. But once that commitment is made, things have a way of lining up exactly the way they should."

She thought her heart would burst. "Wow. Deep."

"Hey. After the hell I went through to get to this point? No way am I gonna accept that something this good has a downside." His lips tilted. "I swear with everything I have in me, I would never hurt you. That I'm in this for the long haul. You gotta believe that."

"I do," she said, knowing beyond a shadow of a doubt she could trust this man with everything she had in her.

Looking vastly relieved, Noah tangled his fingers through her hair, then snorted. "This really is a mess, you know that?"

"And to think some fools actually pay to get this look."

Laughing again, he kissed her forehead. "Marry me? Have my kids? Be my sparring partner for the next sixty or so years?"

She paused, skimming her knuckles across his naked chest. Oh, my. "This mean I have to learn how to cook?"

"Only if you want to, honey. Or I will. Or, hell, we'll hire someone to cook for us. Will you just answer the damn question?"

"Yes," she whispered, grinning so hard she half feared her face would freeze that way. "Yes. Yes, yes, *yes.*"

"Right answer," Noah said, kissing her again. "Now

about that coffee...?" he said, and she laughed and wrapped a sheet around her to pad into the kitchen, where she soon discovered—when Noah folded her into his arms from behind as she filled the basket—exactly how much fun one can have while waiting for the coffee to brew.

Eyes on the prize, cupcake....

And here it was, right in her kitchen.

Heh.

Epilogue

Two days before Christmas, three years later

Noah quietly let himself inside the new, still mostly unfurnished house on the outskirts of Austin, taking a moment to savor the soon-to-be-shattered peace before hanging his keys on a hook by the front door too high for eager little hands to reach. From the back of the house he heard his wife's low laugh, his little girl's high-pitched giggling. Contentment spreading through his chest, he shuffled through a maze of stuffed toys and board books and discarded juice cartons to peer down a hallway already adorned with jelly fingerprints and crayon graffiti. "Hey! Where're my girls?"

"Daddy! Daddy!"

Soft brown curls bouncing, Phoebe barreled toward Noah as fast as her little thunder thighs could manage, squealing when he snatched her into his arms and swung her around.

It never got old, Noah thought, his heart squeezing at her laughter, her absolute trust that he wouldn't let her fall. "Hey, Pheebs—you ready to go see Gramma and Papa? And Uncle Charley and Aunt Edie?"

Securely seated in the crook of his elbow, Phoebe nodded vigorously, her mouth puckered out in her "serious" expression. Noah quickly kissed that irresistible little mouth, then rubbed noses with his daughter. "Where's Mama?"

"Right here," Roxie said, rubbing her six-months-pregnant belly as she entered the room, lifting her face for Noah's kiss. When he pulled away far sooner than, no doubt, either of them would have liked, she arched one brow. "That the best you can do?"

"With a two-year-old in my arms? I'm thinking yes. You all packed?"

"We are, believe it or not. Even if a certain party—" she leveled a mock stern gaze at their daughter "—was determined to take *all* of her 'friends' with her. Did you talk to your folks?" she asked, anticipation twinkling in her eyes. "Is there snow?"

"They're predicting it for tomorrow, so it's looking good for a white Christmas."

"Yay!" Roxie said, taking the slightly puzzled baby into her arms and dancing around the cluttered floor with her for a moment before letting her down to go wreak even more havoc. Definitely her daddy's kid. Then Rox sighed. "Can't tell you how much I'm looking forward to this week."

"Although you do realize between my folks and yours, you might not see our daughter the entire time?"

She grinned. "As I said. So, can I have the rest of my kiss now?"

"I think that can be arranged," Noah said, pulling her as close as their gestating little boy would allow, the kiss this time nice and slow and lingering…until Phoebe decided to sing her version of "Jingle Bells" at the top of her lungs. While jumping on Roxie's cream leather sofa.

Noah laughed. "Kid's gonna fit right in."

"Which she's not going to do if we miss our flight," Rox said, pulling away.

Tugging her close again, Noah murmured, "We've got time."

Even so, he thought—through the next kiss, and the one after that—he was champing at the bit, too, to get back. Even if only for a visit. Although Austin had been damn good to both of them—Noah's fledgling renovation business was taking off, due in no small part, Noah was sure, to the advice he sought from his father on a regular basis, and Rox was still having a blast with the store—even his big city gal had to admit there really was no place like home. So for two weeks every summer and a week at Christmas, they trekked back to recharge, reconnect, remind themselves what was important. Not, Noah thought as he palmed his wife's belly, that they really needed reminding.

"Was he a good boy today?"

"You kidding? He's a Garrett. Hasn't stopped moving all day. I fully expect him to yell 'Charge!' when he comes out."

"You ready for that?"

With a sly, sexy curve of her mouth, Roxie pulled out of his arms and slowly backed away. "Hey. After breaking you in? This one'll be a piece of *cake*—! Noah, no!" she shrieked, reduced to helpless gales of laughter when he caught her and mercilessly attacked her extremely sensitive neck.

"Breaking me in?"

Breathless, still laughing, she grabbed his shoulders and grinned up at him, her curls a jumble around her face. "And what would you call it?"

"Saving my life?" he said softly, watching something melt in her eyes.

Smiling, she knuckled his cheek. "Same here," she whispered, then turned to their daughter. "Come on, sweetie," she said to their little jumping bean. "Time to go!"

"On airp'ane?"

"On airplane, yep! So let's go potty and get our coats...."

As Rox and a chattering Phoebe disappeared down the hall, Noah scanned his chronically messy living room, his gaze lighting on the big-screen TV as he tried to remember the last time he'd watched a DVD all the way through. Or been able to walk around the house naked.

Or what he thought he'd been so afraid of.

His old life? History.

But his new one?

Rox and Pheebs reappeared, Phoebe rolling a Dora the Explorer backpack behind her, and Roxie glanced over and winked at him.

A little piece of heaven.

* * * * *

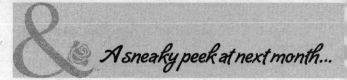

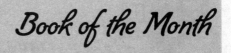

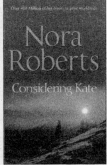

Have Your Say

You've just finished your book. So what did you think?

We'd love to hear your thoughts on our 'Have your say' online panel
www.millsandboon.co.uk/haveyoursay

- 🌹 Easy to use
- 🌹 Short questionnaire
- 🌹 Chance to win Mills & Boon® goodies